DEVOID

A Novel

Greg Sigley

Copyright © 2016. All Rights Reserved.

This is a work of fiction. Names, characters, places, and events are either the product of the author's imagination or are used fictitiously; any resemblance to actual persons, living or dead, businesses, companies, or locales is purely coincidental.

For no moment destroys as harshly and completely as the one when the heart and mind become strangers.

∞

4:48AM, Monday

Save yourself.

Save yourself. I don't think that you are going to be able to save me.

If that sounds a little too dramatic for you, then maybe it's time for you to walk away. This isn't going to be something that you want to hear. I'm used to it, and at times probably play the victim too often, but only in terms of the life I live within. I'll survive. Or maybe not. There's been a lot of drama in my life—no, in my head lately. It's probably of my own doing, at least some of it. Most of it. I tend to think of my life as a movie. There's no denying that. It's hard to turn the thoughts off. Too many—too few. It's always wrong in someone else's eyes. My eyes.

I look to my right to see that I am alone. There's no reason to check the left. It's going to be the same story. Who am I even talking to? Some invisible, made up audience that hangs on every word coming from my mouth? I wish I could say that that is the first time, but I always wanted to be famous. Famous for anything really. It's stupid, unrealistic, a dream as farfetched as traveling to Pluto.

-It's always gonna be a planet to me, I say aloud. Ha!

Just another millennial who thinks they have what it takes to make it big in big Hollywood. Or New York. Hollywood seems so antiquated now. Ha! Antiquated? Look at me using big words to impress an imaginary group of people that probably don't care, either.

-The water looks so black tonight, don't you think? I ponder.

-We really shouldn't be here, you know?

-What does it matter? I lean my head over and listen to the sound of liquid hitting stone. Some of it reaches my cheek, but only a little.

It won't matter in the morning.

-Think I can jump down to that rock there?

A long, flat surface stands somewhat below the one on which I currently find myself. Ten feet? Maybe eight.

-What do you think? One last performance? My body begins to shake. First, and last.

If I can't be the star, maybe I can at least be the sideshow. People enjoy the sideshow, right? They don't come to see them, but they do take pleasure in them. That's what I could be! A sideshow oddity.

Somehow, that doesn't help. It doesn't make me feel better. In fact, there's little comfort in the thought of being a freak. Yet, I feel I have taken on the title.

-Why am I so damn dramatic?

Asinine; it's so fucking asinine. This headspace is nothing more than one over-the-top tragedy after the next. I suppose I should have been Greek. Ha! That's not even funny, but I can't stop laughing tonight. Some people would think that's sick, but my sense of humor has also teetered on the side of gallows.

The cool air surrounds and picks up speed and—Oomph. Okay, that jump was a little higher than I thought.

-Damn it, that hurt!

I rub my ankle and my own howls echo back and forth in the canyon. Who knows whether it's from the pain or the sheer ridiculousness of the situation. What is going on with me tonight? Stupid body. Maybe this is the best decision. I don't know how my body will feel in 20 years if it's giving up already. The shirt tourniquet around my hand begins to loosen and I pull it tight once again. I can't even feel the pain anymore.

-You gave up on me earlier than I expected, body.

Apparently, I feel the need to reiterate this and continue: I can't blame you, though. I haven't exactly been that easy on you over the years. What's some more pain? It's almost over, right?

Am I playing 20 questions with myself? No one else here to ask, I suppose. I just need to hear the words aloud. Make sure that I have made the right decision. It hurts to pull off my boat shoe, but the cold water feels good on my foot. Was that a leaf? Or gross, a fish? Why was that so funny to me?

-So what do you want to talk about? It's been awhile since we've talked, AJ. What have you been up to all these years? Did you move on to some other guy that needed you more? I guess I moved on first, didn't I?

-You'll sink like a rock when you hit the water, he offers up while making a circle in the water with his hand.

-You're an asshole, you know that? I'm not sure if I've ever realized that before.

-I'm just trying to make simple conversation. It's best that you know it's not going to be the immediate peace that you are hoping it's going to be.

-Yeah, I know.

-And if you go to Hell?

I don't answer. My hands begin to tingle and my stomach drops.

-You didn't want to hear it aloud? Isn't that why you are talking to me? You want to run all this by me?

-It pisses me off that you know my thoughts.

-Okay.

-Fuck you, dude!

His chuckle annoys me; I close my eyes and he's gone.

I run my hand through the water. It's cool, refreshing. There's a sense that I'm actually alive. I'm not part of the Matrix. I have always had a weird fascination with water. I guess it's fitting this is how I would want to go. My heart beats heavier against my insides; my chest is tightening, my fingers numb.

-Don't think too much about it. You won't do it if you think it through. You're not strong enough.

Strong enough? It's a move of cowardice in general public opinion. That's what I thought for a long time, but I've never been to this point before. I've never felt like I was losing control of my own mind or my own emotions. There's no peace in being awake. There's no freedom that comes with age. Just a larger cage made of paper requiring everything I've ever earned.

The pain doesn't stop. High school repeats itself over and over under pseudonyms like office politics. Invisible knives constantly find themselves sticking from my back. Little things build into more than they should and eventually you just want out.

-I just want out.

I wonder if anyone will come to the service. Even now, my vanity finds its way through to the surface. Is it so wrong to wonder if people actually care? They usually don't when it comes to those currently in their lives. I'm guilty of it, too. Maybe, I should leave something about what I want. Maybe I should just tell my mom not to do anything. It would save her money. The best thing that can happen is if they can't find the body.

-Body.

Saying it out loud doesn't have the effect that I thought it might. Still, there's no realness to the word. My chest begins to tighten again. Not sure if it ever unfurled from the first bout of anxiety upon arrival at this spot.

-Stop.

Stop thinking about it. You have to be stronger than this at least. Be stronger than yourself. Don't be a coward and disappoint your entire life. It's almost over, so just be brave about it. Let them know you did it on your own terms.

They'll be sad. They'll talk. There will always be talk; that never ceases to be true. They'll say horrible things. Will they wonder about the times that they abandoned me? Will they wonder about the times that they blew me off? Or the times I blew them off. Look at me, feeling sorry for myself again.

-Climb off the burn pile, Joan of Arc, you're no martyr.

Maybe I deserve to be blown off, to be ignored? I play the victim all the time. You can't go through life doing that; people will start to blame you. They will start to hate you. Resent you for letting it happen over and over again.

-Stop laughing! It's not that funny, AJ! Why do I even talk to you? Do you think I'm a monster?

There I go, again, apologizing for my feelings. I shouldn't have to apologize for how I'm feeling, for being the person that I am. I don't remember the last time that I felt something for someone else, though. My empathy hit a wall years ago, but I don't think there's really one moment that could be pinpointed for the end of that era.

Another person, I mean. Animals, that's where my heart lies. They need me. They need someone in their corner because the world is such an awful place. People think that it's okay to throw them away. It's not.

-What is your problem? Go away. I have my own thoughts in my head, and I don't need yours. Get away from me! I won't let another person do this to me, let alone someone like you! I'm already done! Just stop, just leave me alone! AJ, get the fuck out of here. I don't need your friendship anymore!

-You're overreacting. And—you might be losing your mind.

-You don't think I know that? Go.

I feel myself falling backwards but I have no way to stop it. The base of my neck collides against a surface with no give and the pain is immediate, however numbed by the liquor. My head aches, but only for a moment. I pick up the bottle and pull it to my lips. The liquid spills over the lower part of my face as I try to find my mouth. It doesn't taste good, but the warmth in my chest makes up for the brief, unsavory taste. Only a matter of time now. Is this something that needs to be dramatic, or is it something that I should just do and be done? I suppose the whole act is dramatic.

There I go again. Drama. I'm so stupid. Just so damn stupid. There doesn't need to be drama. I'm sure that is what ruined most of the friendships that I had, the need to be the center of attention. It happened even when I didn't understand it myself. I used to be the life of the party, the crazy one that everyone wanted to be around. They wanted to spend time with me, but as we age, that goes away. It turns into a problem that no one really understands. Hell, I don't even understand it fully. I just know that sometimes you have to fight your demons, even if you know they are going to win.

What is it they say about the brightest star burning out faster? Does the star even know that is the risk of putting itself in that position?

This time, they've won. I know that I've come to the point that I can't go on doing the same old thing. I can't make it work. I've tried over and over again. I've prayed, I've hoped; I've made comments about it. No one cares. They tell me it's not funny.

I never meant it to be. There was some part of me that needed the help, needed someone to step in and understand, to tell me that it's not okay. No one stepped in, made a plea. So, here we are. I am finally making the ultimate decision that this has to stop. I have to stop. I have no more will power to pretend that I'm going to be alright.

-I'm never going to be alright.

I've made my decision; if I hadn't already, I should say. I love so many people, but they never loved me. This could completely be on me, I recognize. I was always the option they had if nothing better came along. I'm tired of being an option.

Is it too much to want someone to care for me? For me, not for someone that I pretended to be. Pretending to be someone that you never were takes its toll on the mind. Eventually, you're not even sure who you are, or were, and everything is one big damn mess. Who cares, really? If they really thought about me, even for one brief moment, would I have made it this far? To the point where I can say goodbye so easily. There's no use trying to be strong any longer; it seems it has mostly been in vain.

-My loneliness is killing me, I laugh.

You can only deal with being told that you are not good enough for so long. Eventually, that is the mentality that you understand, that you live with. It's a mentality that overtakes and becomes who you are.

-Hey man, you okay?

-AJ?

-Uh, no.

I turn around, squinting to find a face for the voice but can only see a small orange glow in the darkness.

-What's so funny?

His voice sounds vaguely West Coast, slightly nasal, a lot *bro.*

-What do you mean, I ask.

-You were laughing. Kinda loud, dude. What's so funny? Let me in on the joke.

-Sorry if I bothered you.

-You didn't. Now, what the fuck were you laughing at?

-Whoa.

-Sorry, I meant that to be funny. You don't know me, though. Probably shouldn't come off harsh to someone I just met in the middle of the night. Morning? I'm so fucking high. Now come on, what made you laugh so hard?

-It's weird, I have no idea. I don't even remember.

-Are you high, too?

-No, drunk.

He laughed. The sound of this put me at ease. I'm totally high, he announced. Mind if I sit down, he continued.

-Nah, go for it.

-I'm Matt.

-Ezra.

-Never actually met an Ezra before. Nice to meet you.

He holds out his hand, and I take it quickly. It was light and quick. He lay back on the rock and I start to make out a few facial features. Well, what I assume is a beard or a weirdly misshapen jaw. I can't imagine he would have a broken jaw and be outside wandering around tonight, though. Or, that could be exactly the type of person that wonders around in the woods in the middle of the night.

-What are you doing out here, he asks.

-Just thinking—and drinking. The water is peaceful.

-Are you out here alone?

-Why? Thinking of robbing me, I say with a smile that I cannot lose.

-You caught me, sir. I can barely stand, but I will definitely be robbing you.

-Considering how drunk I am, I'm sure it would be pretty equal and a real shitshow. But no, it's just me. You?

I realize that I probably should have lied to him. I don't really want to end up beaten and—dead. There's a ridiculousness in that way of thinking in this situation that brings on another roar.

-Dude, either stop laughing or let me in on the joke! It's driving me crazy!

-Nothing, just the beer talking, or thinking. I'm not even making sense to myself tonight. What brings you out here?

-Just in, rafting and camping for the weekend with some buddies of mine. We saw it was going to be warm and decided to take advantage of it.

-Where are they?

-Passed out. Too much to drink for them, too. See the fire over there?

I assume that he is pointing through the trees, but I can't be sure. There's a soft glow that might be a fire, but I can't really say for sure. Could just be the power of persuasion. My eyes have become glazed, and the exhaustion set in hours ago. I feel like my eyes should have adjusted to the night by now, but the clouds continue to cover and uncover the moon in frequent patterns, making it far more difficult to decipher anything fully. It's not something I would have ever noted had its existence not been pointed out.

-Yeah, I mutter.

Agreeing is the easiest thing to do right now; I don't have the energy for him to keep trying to point out something that really doesn't matter, anyway.

-Where are you from, I ask.

-Texas.

Damn, I think. I was wrong.

-But I grew up in California, he continues. Southern Cali.

I was right. I like being right. Who doesn't?

-What about you, sir?

-It doesn't matter. The Midwest is pretty much all the same.

-You out here for vacation?

-Nah, moved here a few years ago.

-That's awesome! I've been here the last few weeks hanging out, but I've thought about moving. It's so beautiful. Almost supernatural. Ya know?

The full intoxication has taken over his voice, a losing battle against the sound of the falling water. I should not have assumed that it was a cigarette. Not here, in the middle of the night. It's kind of a known hippie spot. The distinct smell should have tipped me off, but my good friend, whiskey, has reduced my senses to superficial at best.

-That sounded really douchey, didn't it, he asks me, and for once, I can see his eyes glimmer in the moonlight.

-No, I know what you're talking about.

Again, I don't want to argue or extend the conversation. Too tired; too wasted.

-This may just be the weed, dude, but you seem like a pretty cool guy.

-Thanks, man.

-It's true! You are probably a pretty awesome human being, he mumbles while failing to sit upright.

-You don't have to say that.

I start laughing again.

-Another joke? He asks.

-No, you. Why would you worry about my opinion? I'm a random guy you met laying on a rock in the middle of the night. I think that you can guess that I'm not a pillar of the community.

-True.

Matt starts with a low chuckle before he loses his cool completely.

-We're a pair, aren't we? He poses.

-What do you mean?

-Two randos in the middle of the night, drunk and one of us very, very high. We have barely discussed anything, but I am ready to Facebook friend you. And, as you know, that is the biggest of deals.

I snicker and his teeth now come into view, white, like his eyes. No brighter. The eyes are dulled by the weed. Tonight's not a great representation for them, although there is really no reason that I should care. He looks young, probably early twenties once the full picture has come together.

-Yes, yes it is, I quip.

He slaps my shoulder. How can someone that I don't even know make me feel like maybe someone in this world does care about me? That's stupid. I'm too easy. Possibly an optimist. Don't let that get out to people. I want to believe that people care about me. Even strangers. Don't second guess yourself now, Ez. He's high and you won't ever see him again. You may not see anyone again.

-Fuck, there's no cell service out here, he yells and laughs.

-I think that's probably a good thing for camping. Ya know? People like to get away. Be alone.

-Yeah, true. I have never been like that, though. I'm better when I have an audience, when people are around to talk to. Solitude is not my forte, dude.

-I used to think it was mine, but there are days now that I'm not so sure. An audience can be nice, but in the end, do they really care?

-Wow, this just got serious.

-Sorry, didn't mean to put that out there so bluntly.

-I'm kidding, it's fine. No worries, man. Want a hit off this?

I can see the white paper in front of my face and think for a moment before I take it between my fingers. The smell encompasses any sobriety that might be left floating in my head. Thanks, man, I say.

-No problem. Let's have a good night, sir. I'm wide awake, and I'm guessing you are, too.

-Ya know, I have absolutely no idea what time it is. Might be morning.

-Oh, that's a fact.

-I would probably be getting up for work then.

-You off today?

-No.

-Ah.

A languid tightness has found its way from my body into some other form for which I cannot explain, but it's no longer with me. Is this God? Did he send this crazy hippie out here to keep me distracted until I could think clearly? This high off of his ass stranger? I laugh at the irony at this supposition, but God does work in mysterious ways as everyone puts it.

I am thinking clearly.

Is he supposed to make me feel better about the decision that I've made or change my mind? Why has life become so difficult? I'm a damn mess and I just can't seem to make it work out. Why is my head so fucked up? I just want everything to work out for once.

It does work out. You don't appreciate it like you should.

Is that so much to ask? Is it me; is it the world?

Josh.

Don't.

-Where'd you go, dude?

-Huh? Just thinking, sorry. It's been a long night.

-I kinda picked up on that, he laughs.

My hand brushes over the rough surface intermittently confirming many misses of the bottle I seek. Finally, the smooth glass is found and I breathe out heavily. I can't even really taste it anymore.

-Can I get some of that?

-Sure.

I hand him the bottle and listen as he gulps loudly. Normally that would annoy me, but my body has found its way into some weird state of nirvana. I'm no expert on the subject, but a drug and alcohol induced nirvana is nothing like the actual meaning.

Is there such a thing as bro at first sight? Ha! Matt's breathing is slow, but steady, and it's nice to have someone here. No words, just here.

-Well, that goes down pretty easily, doesn't it? Matt says aloud after several minutes of silence.

-It's the good stuff; decided not to skimp tonight.

My voice sounds deeper, cooler, unrecognizable. Sleep had nearly taken hold for the night before he had chimed in and brought the force of reality back.

-Hell yeah, it is!

-Haven't even felt the need to vom! This was louder than intended, but I'm sure Matt couldn't tell the difference.

-Well—that's good then.

I hear him gulp down more.

-Slow down there, killer, I say.

Killer? I have never in my life used that phrase, but it definitely came out of my mouth.

He laughs.

-Sorry, just so good. So. Good.

-I think we already established that, bro.

-Smart ass.

I reach over and grab the bottle from him, almost violently. The heat from Matt's fingers finds its way up my arm and into my chest. The invigorating burn from another gulp meets the heat in my chest and works its way into my stomach. How long do you think it takes to get from my mouth to my stomach? Should I grab my phone and time the sensation? Nah, too tired. Also, that might be the stupidest thought I’ve ever had. A small chuckle passes through my lips but quickly dissipates.

There are few spots on the rock that the bottle can sit comfortably without falling. The realization that I have had too much should have occurred earlier in the evening, but the pull at my tear ducts that I might not have any more is the final straw. My judgement on time is off, but the length of time I hold onto the bottle to avoid disaster is prolonged and unnecessary. I could finish it. Should I do that? Would that be rude? I don’t know him and it’s mine, so I guess it really doesn’t matter. What if he beats the shit out of me? It would save me some trouble, I guess.

I move my arm slowly, letting my fingers meet his. He pulls away. The pull seems to be more of a surprise than one of disdain. It was quick, not cold, not unfeeling.

-What are you doing?

-I’m so sorry, dude. This shit has me all out of it tonight. Really, I’m sorry. I’m truly a fucking moron.

-No, it’s fine.

He takes another drag of his joint and continues: are you okay?

-Honestly?

-Yeah.

-No.

He grabs the back of my neck.

Fuck, he is going to beat the shit out of me. Matt places his other hand and my own on his chest.

-It's going to be okay, Ezra whatever your last name is. It is.

12:45AM, Sunday

Just one more drink. That's all you need Ez. You're drunk, and blacking out is not what you want to do tonight.

No more alienating friends. You don't know how much longer they are going to put up with it, and you don't like yourself when you get like this. This could be the main reason going out alone feels like a better choice for me at times. If I alienate a stranger, who cares, right? Just more faces in the crowd that most likely will not cross my path again. There's no reason people should be seen like this, as disposable. I'm not a sociopath, but I don't want to be hurt again. Everyone has feelings; everyone has a soul. I should care more about them.

It's difficult for me to account for that most of the time because I am selfish. I'm a narcissist. Which is worse, being one or knowing that you are one and not caring? It's not that I want to be this selfish, but I am, and I can't seem to stop. What should be a normal conversation leads me on a journey back to my own needs and wants. I don't just want that to be done, I need it to be.

-What the fuck am I doing?

-What?

The bartender looks at me like I've lost my mind and there's a realization that I have said this out loud.

-Did you need something, he asks, subtly annoyed.

-Yeah, can I get a Redbull vodka, I ask.

He raises an eyebrow and pulls a glass from an unseen shelf behind the bar. The minutes have lost all urgency, and the multiple conversations are nothing but background noise in the spinning of my head. Some insipid comment makes me laugh to myself as my eyes follow the movements of the bartender, carefully judging the pour to make sure it meets my own requirements.

-Thanks, I say and strut back to my friends, who are each seated around a long table in the far corner of the restaurant.

My friend's voices have joined those of the strangers, no particular story standing out above another, so I sip my drink and smile. There's no reason to believe that they had the slightest idea that I'd left. It's in their nature, my nature, to not pay a lot of attention to what is going on elsewhere in a room. Occasionally, I throw in a nod to make them think I agree with whatever it is they're clamoring on about.

That's the general M.O. until the rolling blackout sets in, anyway. It's not healthy, but it's what it is, so yeah. The need for friends escapes me at the moment.

I'm that guy at the end of the night that you want to avoid like the plague because it's hard to tell what kind of a tangent I might get on. Drinking numbs the pain that for some reason my body insists on feeling. I have tried so much to get rid of it, replace it with nothingness, but for some reason it creeps back in and eats at me until there's no choice but to acknowledge it. Then I drink, and I drink a lot. And then drink more. It's common knowledge that this is not the best way to handle it, but I'm a cliché. Can't deny that. Everyone is, in one sense of the word or another.

-Where is Katie? I hear one of the girls ask.

-She's on the way, or so she says. Margaret answers the question pointedly, but she's right.

Margaret types something on her phone and puts it back in her coat pocket.

-Did she say how long, I ask?

-Ten minutes, but you know how she is!

-So an hour, I add loudly.

We all laugh. It's easy to pretend that I have always been one of them, but the truth is, it took a lot of acting. Taking cues from the way they look, talk, act, and the people that they hang out with. It's not really that it's all a lie, but I have learned from the mess that was high school that if you don't fit in somewhere, life is going to be somewhat of a nightmare. It's preferential to have people that will have your back, even if you only see them once in a while.

Being me is not acceptable. I'm too weird, too—I dunno, but it's never enough. Maybe it's all in my mind; I've never been the one that anyone wanted or cared about. I'm the additional wheel; the third, fifth, twelfth. Here I am, though, feeling sorry for myself, yet standing tall next to them. There are times I feel that I can be alone, but it seems to actually be a struggle for me.

There's a chronic need for affection that looms just below the surface, and I need the attention to be solely on me. The warmth of another human, even just the proximity, can push away the sense of loneliness that can center on one's soul.

The conversation. Is it even really the conversation? I like it when they listen. If they could hear what I think, they would assume that there's a sort of madman in there. Not violent, but not someone with whom they would be happy to associate. I'm sure they already think that.

-Yes! I love this song! I shout and everyone looks.

My torso moves back and forth, my hand working adamantly to not spill my drink, but I'm unsuccessful. I put it down on the table and bounce up and down to the beat. I do have a little rhythm still leftover from teen dances far too many years past to recall each one with a numeral. Everyone laughs. It's the response I hope for, I guess. Pay attention, smile, let me know that you care.

It all feels so false, though. I do what I can, but in the end, I am not going to ever be the first thing on their minds. Is there a person somewhere that has been here, that can tell me it gets easier? Always being an afterthought. Of course there is someone. Where would the world be without the depressing songs about being alone? Oh, life, you are something.

Their friend at the end of the table is cute. She twists her hair around her finger and laughs, letting her whole body fall into small convulsions. No, don't think that. It's stupid. I'm definitely not the type of guy that she would pay any attention. There's been no indication of an attraction; she hasn't even looked this way. Her eyes inadvertently scan Nick's chest before she finds her gaze back on Margaret. Of course.

Why am I even thinking about this? It's supposed to be a good night. Shots. That's a good way to keep it going. Forget the worry; enjoy right now.

Katie approaches the table quickly, throwing her black purse over the back of the only empty seat. I grab her hand and say:

-You're late.

She presses her forehead against mine and smiles.

-I know, I couldn't get away from work, I had so much—, she starts.

-Let's get a drink; you need to catch up.

-Let me put my coat down.

Her dark hair bunches up around her head and neck as she hugs each member of the group. Yeah, just put down your coat. It's a few minutes before she finds her way back to me and says that she is ready for that drink.

-Let's do it then. My response is sarcastic but hopefully not noticeable.

I grab her soft hand and lead her to the bar.

-Two shots of tequila, I command loudly five steps before we actually touch the wooden top.

-Salt and lime, the bartender asks and smiles. He may have winked, but I could just be buzzed. In fact, that's the most likely scenario. It's nice to be noticed. No matter whom it is.

I look to Katie for her answer and watch the wrinkles appear on her forehead and her chin lift with her eyes as she nods slightly. Maybe it's too early in the evening, but what the hell. The answer:

-Yeah, please.

My gaze finds Katie quickly.

-How was work?

-It was good. The usual. How are you, love?

-Eh, you know!

She laughs and I reach for the two small glasses of clear liquid that have been placed in front of us. She gets the first before my hand grabs the second. I don't know why but I let the odor linger under my nose before the glass finds its way to my lips. This is generally not the best idea; any person that drinks knows this to be true. The receipt gets my signature before my hand grabs the yellow-tinted drink that I have had refilled to take back to the table.

-Babe, we need to get you a new drink. That was disgusting!

-That's ludicrous!

She laughs.

-I hate you so much!

-I know. I hate me, too!

Her kiss on my cheek feels warm, familiar, and loving; she then wraps her arm inside of mine like they are pieces of a puzzle.

I've completely fallen away from whatever they have been talking about at this point, but it's not something to which I care to put my thought tonight. This is the beginning of what I assume will become a mess. It's late and if we are going to get drunk, we gotta make this happen now. My head is slowly fogging over, and I smile. The bottom of my glasses rises high into the air, a spectacle and sign that the drink is about to come to its conclusion and the show will begin shortly. I'm too old for this. I know that, but it's fun. It can be fun.

-What are you all doing on Thursday, Lindsay shouts down the table; a domino effect of silence falls over the table until it finally reaches me. She pulls at her low-cut top and repeats the question.

-Are you asking all of us, Melissa finally answers after a moment of confused, and continued, silence.

-Yes! She laughs.

-Why, what's going on?

-Well, I got this Groupon for ballroom dancing, and I thought you guys might want to try it with me?

The quiet calmness now becomes a fearful pit in the stomachs of each person at the table; scrunched faces do not hide the truth. I'm sure she can tell. She has to be able to tell if I can. I'm drunk, for fuck's sake.

-Come on, I think it's going to be fun!

-Umm, well, Nick started.

Thankfully, the waitress made her entrance, like she had realized what was about to happen to all of us and wanted to somehow save the day. Supergirl. Ha! I should tip her more; she deserves it for ending this conversation. This would-be debacle.

-Is there anything else I can get for anyone, she inquired in a smoky voice twenty years the senior of her body and face.

-Yeah, could we get our checks, Nick chimes in as soon as the question ends.

-Oh, come on! Lindsay screams. Ez?

-I actually have to work late on Thursday, I stutter.

-You're lying.

-Okay, I don't want to go ballroom dancing.

-Really?

-Also, I'm poor.

-You came out tonight.

-This meal is the only one I'm getting this week. The group laughs, even Lindsay through her flippant, angry face. I'm not totally sure the touch of rage in her eyes was for show, though.

Our waitress is standing at a POS system in the opposite corner of our table slowly typing in each order. She stops, places the leather pads on the counter and pulls her hair into a loose bun. She continues poking in the numbers and returns ten minutes later with each check, separated. Her eyes and disheveled hair show annoyance, but her mouth paints a picture of joy. Joy to serve those around her and hopefully the happiness of a large tip from a group our size.

I scan the check to see if a gratuity has already been added, which is standard for a group this size in many establishments. There is none, and I try to figure out 20 percent of the total. My brain is not functioning the way it should, only slightly because of my exhaustion, so I leave closer to 25 percent. It's much easier just to divide the total by four, even for a hazy brain.

Everyone is standing from the table to move toward the back room, the "club" part of the restaurant. I don't even think it's a part of the restaurant, just a shared door placed for whatever reason long before either business was conceived. The word Tanzen blurs my retina in neon just above the entrance. We enter, pushing through bodies; it seems early for this amount of excitement, but I haven't checked the time recently. There are no faces, just torsos and legs.

Our group stops at the end of another long, wooden surface and I push through the middle of them to lean against the wall. I love this song, and my body begins to move.

-You okay, Katie whispers into my ear.

The question barely lingers before it's gone and I watch the way the green and blue lights spin around on Melissa's blonde hair. She's sitting diagonal from me and takes a drink from a rocks glass. The drink doesn't look familiar, but a pineapple rests over the lip of the cup. The light on her hair looks cool, like water, and then I realize it's probably just the alcohol that is making it appear so fascinating. Katie leans in closer and asks another question, one I feel like I am hearing wrong.

-Huh, I ask. My head almost hits here in surprise, but I need to be sure.

-You look cute tonight, she repeats.

-Uh, thanks.

She grabs my hand as my friends talk on in front of us. What are you doing, I ask.

-Just let it happen, she says, laughing.

-You're drunk.

-So are you.

-True.

-What are you two laughing about? Lindsay yells near my face.

-Nothing, I say quietly, and I feel my hand begin to sweat.

-What? She bellows, as if more volume will make her slurring comprehensive.

-Nothing!

-Let's get a drink, she shouts and waves her half full glass in front of my face. She chugs the remainder of the amber liquid and her green eyes find mine. I can't help but laugh, shake my head, and move in front of her to lead her through the crowd.

My fingers slowly fall away from Lindsay's softer digits as Melissa moves into our path.

-Where are you going, she asks from a small divide between us and the door to the restaurant.

-Another drink.

-There's a bar right here, she points out, confused as to what is happening.

-We want it from that bar, I point to the one in the back of the room surrounded by people.

-That's stupid. Get it here.

-We don't—I trail off, and sigh heavily before continuing: We want to go over there where all the action is. No one is over here.

I stop moving towards the bar for a moment when I realize that Lindsay is talking to Ray. She pushes her hand through his gelled hair and he moves back quickly while she laughs. She kisses him on the cheek, loving, sweet. I miss that. At this point, I can't even remember the last time that I even wanted that with someone that has come into my life. That feeling of being in love or even just *liking* someone. I sound like I am in fifth grade now. *Like?* Wow, I really must be drunk. I'm telling the truth to myself.

-You ready? Lindsay asks.

-Yeah, let's go.

I can *almost* hear myself sigh as I use my shoulder to push through the crowd. It's tight, it's loud, it's a nightclub. We traverse the maze, bobbing my head to the music. Everyone is dancing, but they aren't listening to the words. They're sad. This person is dying inside while smiling. Always smiling. You can only drink and dance your pain away for so long before there's nothing left. Just memories and sadness. Shut up. Just shut up. We push into the miniscule spot between two stools and I speak immediately.

-Ginger ale and whiskey, and what do you want, I turn and ask Lindsay.

- Uh, hang on. Her eyes move intently back and forth across the illuminated bottles like she is reading the menu at a fast food restaurant.

Now, there's no coming down from this high. But, no there's no feeling alive—I need to remember these lyrics. Remember these lyrics; download it later. My phone reaches the bar top when I meet the glare of the bartender and turn once again to Lindsay.

-Hey, he's waiting. Do you know what you want?

- Just get me something sweet.

-Let me get a Kamikaze for her, I lean in and speak loudly as the song disappears into another.

The cologne he's wearing seems familiar but I can't place it. Someone I knew, or know, wears the same scent. It's not important, but it digs at my memory. He stops and rolls his sleeves up, tight against his defined arms before adjusting the sweat band around his arm that holds the silver bottle opener.

Now there's no coming back down from this high. But there's no feeling alive.

Remember those lyrics. Search for them later. Get the song. I pull my wallet from my back pocket. It's harder these days than it used to be. Jeans are tighter and everything is a bit saggy. You're too old for this. You can't drink like this anymore. The drink is more bitter than sweet. Good, it's the way I like it. I hand Lindsay her drink just before handing my debit card, dinged and worn, to the bartender.

-Thanks, man.

-Yeah, no problem, he answers nonchalantly. It's barely above a whisper and I begin to wonder for a moment if I simply read his lips and the sound was all in my head.

We are just more faces in the crowd, another customer. A possible tip, a possible mess, but then it ends around 2:30. He won't remember most, if any, of the people that he served. It's a piece of intangible artwork, a Picasso. Features from one blending into another. It's all just finite. I can't help but laugh at myself. Might as well be a freshman in Art History, but then it's all gone from my head. All these words, these thoughts; sometimes it would just be nice for them to all stop. Sleep. That's the medicine I need.

There's something about a face that stays with me long past an initial meeting, and I think I would do well as a bartender; it could be fun. My mind has a knack for grappling onto knowledge that I don't need and holding it far past a normal, expected expiration date. I can see a face a year later and remember something inane, such as the last four numbers of their phone number. This unusual trick has caused more than one side-glance over the years upon mentioning some random fact most would pretend they didn't know or remember.

He motions with the card across his neck and I nod. He turns back to the small black computer screen and pulls the plastic swiftly through the crevice to the left. The process is mechanized from many nights of the same. The nameless man hands the card back to me. Not really a man. He's too young for that but not a boy, either. Somewhere around twenty-five, maybe.

For a moment, there's a tinge of angst, or jealousy, that I'm no longer at the same point in my life. It hasn't been that many years since, but my body feels like it is starting to count down instead of up. This isn't something that's socially acceptable to question out loud at my age, as I'm sure anyone 10, or even 20, years older than me would look at me like I am losing my mind.

There's no denying that the aches come swifter and stay longer now. Should have done more with my life. Some people my age are millionaires. Needless to say, I am not one of those success stories. Lindsay looks at me as I sigh deeply and smile.

-Thanks again, dude, he says as I take the leather-bound folder from him, discern an amount for the tip, and sign my name at the bottom of the long white paper. It's become even harder to decide what the actual tip should be due to my decreased capacity for addition, so I tip higher even higher than the previous bill. He seemed nice enough. I crumple the receipt; why are they so long anyway? Too much useless information at the bottom. Who reads it?

-Thanks for the drink, Lindsay yells.

-Dial back the volume there, crazy! I laugh; but really, she spit on me when she bellowed. The group could have heard her.

-Sorry! I think maybe I need to stop after this one!

-That's quitter talk, Linds. Do you want to be known as a quitter?

She trips and I catch her arm before her body can fall below the top of the bar. Only a few drops of the sunshine liquid spill from the glass she is carrying.

-You okay, I ask.

-Fine, but I definitely am not going to fall for your peer pressure now!

-Not sure what exactly you were "falling" for there.

She laughs and walks back to stand beside Ray. Her small arm looks like a child's as she weaves it through his. The muscles in his back tense before realizing who it is that has invaded his space.

-Where have you been, Katie asks and puts her arm around my waist when I rejoin the group seconds after Lindsay.

-At the bar. I take a sip and continue: Feeling pretty good, aren't you?

-Only a little. It's Saturday! What else are we going to do?

-True.

-Or, we could be responsible adults who make a contribution to society instead of representing the delinquent half. But, nah. That sounds very tiring.

I take another long swig of my drink and let the warmth cuddle my heart before it falls like a rollercoaster to my gut. The heat settles here briefly and then it's gone. Ah, that feels nice. The patio twenty feet away looks hazy through the lens of my glass covered in finger prints, presumably, and hopefully, my own. Small piles of snow remain but they are broken up by what would appear to be the brave, or stupid, people that cannot forego a cigarette for the warmth of the bar. It's hard to believe that the temperature outside stands around 50 degrees currently. There is very little that I find myself able to focus on for more than a minute. There's a thought, then there's not. That rhymed. Ha!

It's difficult to distinguish any one voice from another and it's doubtful that the information currently buzzing around is something that I need anyway. There's a very good chance that I won't remember any of this tomorrow. The liquor is too far gone, barely, but too far gone; it's further than I'd planned, but here we are. No looking back, no stopping the dizzying feeling that precedes numb oblivion. Wow, that sounded dark. Just look towards tomorrow. Find that damn star and follow it until morning. Today? Another sip, more warmth.

Melissa's head finds its way to my shoulder, and the warmth from it feels pleasant, but slight. I ask if she's okay and she nods slowly, her hair getting caught against the fabric of my peacoat. Do you want to go sit down, I continue. She nods again. I slowly place my hand at the small of her back and help her lean against the wall before letting her know that we will be moving in a minute. I pull my hand from her body, slowly, and turn to the rest of the group.

-Guys, let's move to that empty booth over there. I don't think Melissa is doing very well.

Melissa is the decision-maker for the group and the fact that she has gotten this drunk is out of the norm. She's usually in control of herself among others.

-Something wrong tonight, Mel, I ask.

-No, I'm fine. Just trying to have a good time for once.

For once?

The position of group lead was self-appointed, but everyone goes along with it. It's not fun all the time, but she's a good person. Her tastes just differ from my own. She thrives on going to the smallest, most expensive places that she can find. Venues with no free parking and walking distances that seem in the mile range. The ones that are trendy for a short time before ultimately shutting down once the fascination passes.

Me? There needs to be room to spread out, to enjoy myself. Too many people make me nervous. Maybe, that's why I drink so much. No, I can't really explain that away. I just love the feeling of being able to lose myself for a little bit.

Lindsay looks around, gauging what the response of the group will be if we shift positions, I assume. She likes to think that she is in charge, but she doesn't like to make an enemy of the rest of the group. It's a fine line to walk, like choosing to marry Henry VIII. Ha! That's the type of joke that has me labeled as weird; too literate, too something. One of many little eccentricities that leave me utterly forgettable amongst those who couldn't care less about English history. It's a fine line that I walk; somewhere between educated and common. Not to say these people are common, but—I dunno.

I won't be forgotten, I can't be.

Why does that matter so much?

Who the hell knows?

Is it so wrong to want to leave something behind that people will remember, something worthy? I don't know what constitutes as worthy, but worthy of someone who matters. It's weird, this need to explain to myself what I feel remembered even means. If I can't be thought of here and now, then maybe in the future. Stupid, I know. I won't be around to see it, but it makes me feel better. I'm not scared of not being here; I'm not scared of death.

That's what I keep telling myself, anyway.

Burn out if that's what you need; the audience loves a good self-destruction.

Maybe I *am* scared. Either way, when it's over, it's over. If there is something left behind, something beautiful, something brilliant, then maybe those who knew of my flaws could forget them. And those who didn't know the truth, would just remember the greatness. It's a degree of what I call the Saint syndrome. People tend to forget the negative qualities of someone they have lost.

It's easy to remember the good, to recollect what you knew from the outside. The truth behind the matter; the flaws, shown to only those near the deceased, are gone. I want to go a step further and leave something that even strangers know as wonderful.

-Yeah, that's fine, Lindsay finally answers, monitoring the looks of our group to make sure that everyone wants to sit.

The decision should have been immediate; the well-being of our friend should come first, before Lindsay's popularity. It's getting late and the concern for how the night is going is one that should be diminished if not altogether gone.

-Come on, Mel, let's go over there and sit down.

-Ok, she mumbles, or slurs. Both.

I nod my head in the direction of the empty booth as she swings her arm around my neck. It feels nice to be needed, even if only in less-than-ideal circumstances. Mel reaches for her drink but Lindsay grabs it first.

-Let me carry that for you, girl, she pipes in and leads the way.

Melissa falls into the booth harder than intended and I mutter an apology that I'm sure she doesn't hear or understand. She immediately reaches for the drink that Lindsay plops on the table as the back of my hand brushes the sweat from my forehead. I'm not sweating profusely but enough that I notice. Does anyone else?

Another drink is in order. The path to the bar seems more difficult in light of the sobriety that seems to be reigniting within my body. The trips for new drinks are innumerable at this point, but it's comforting to see the same face each time. No one knows why I've walked away, if they notice at all. There is no importance in this knowledge and the night will go on with or without my presence.

Damn, it's only 12:45. The time is dragging. My phone must be broken, or behind. When is the time change? We've been here forever. Less than an hour actually. The fun has already subsided. I look back to the table and everyone is laughing.

Not Melissa.

She must have pre-gamed before they picked her up. I'm sure they all did. Part of me is glad that I had to work late; it kept me from ending up like her. That's the state that I would be in if I had gone. That's how the night will end.

The night doesn't have to go that route.

It will.

How else do you end up with a good story? This logic is fucked up, and I know that. In my fantasy world it's easy to pretend that I don't have a problem. Maybe I don't, could just be severe depression. I don't start the day with a beer. Hmm? Mel's state continues to level out my own drunkenness.

Drink. Just keep drinking and have a good time. She'll be fine. We always are.

I don't drink every day, just social events and such. Isn't that what they all say? That's cliché number one in AA.

Think about everyone around you; they don't want to see you obliterated.

They did at one time.

I don't think about my friends enough when we go out, or maybe I do? Too much? My process is to analyze every single angle; what do they want from me? I want to know how it is they are going to hurt me before they do it. They're always going to hurt me. I know that. It's just best to know beforehand, to prepare.

-What can I get for you?

The bartender's eyes seem brighter. Probably just the stupor I'm working towards. Crystal blue. Lines form at the edge of his eyes and his shoulders fall. The names of the liquors are running together. Just tell him what you want. You know exactly what you're going to order, Ezra.

-Whiskey, I mutter. Jameson.

-Any mixer?

-No.

-On the rocks?

-Sure.

Show him that you're a badass. No mixer, no chaser. He doesn't care one way or another as long as I don't cause a scene. Friendlier demeanor means better tip. Don't let him think you're a pussy. Man up and be cool. This moment is the only thing that matters right now. Live in it. He may have said cool but the response was quick, too quick to decipher. He turns and grabs the green bottle behind him and fills the glass of ice; I didn't even see him add the cubes.

-You have a tab?

You know I don't.

My leather wallet poses only minimal issues in its retrieval from the back pocket, and I slip the card into his hand.

-Start one, please, I say and take the drink from the freshly wiped bar.

My disappearance from the group seems to have had very little effect on them. I take a long drink and decide that the next drink should be a double, maybe a triple.

No, that's a terrible idea.

That's how you get cut off real quick. The drinks are fading fast, and so is my sense of caring. How do I get the fun back? Trouble builds when dwelling on my position as the third wheel. There's no use to give it a number anymore. I've been them all. Third, fifth, thirteenth.

Melissa seems to have rebounded in the short span of time that found me absent from her side. I don't know how she did it but now there are smiles and full words where before there had been slurs and tears.

-What happened there, I ask Lindsay, pointing.

-I have no idea. We got her water and she bounced back.

Lindsay reaches for my drink and asks what's in it. She pulls the beverage beneath her nostrils and they flare.

-No, thank you! I dunno how you drink that stuff.

-It's good! It's classy, I say laughing. I go further: I'm old now, and this is what old farts drink.

-Yeah, okay, but keep it over there. I don't want to smell it. It's going to make me puke.

-Oh, it won't be around for too long. Besides, it doesn't even smell that strong.

Another gulp and the liquid is gone. The glass practically falls onto the table with a clank.

-Be right back, looks like I need another.

-You sure about that?

-Worried about me?

-You know I am, she says and kisses my cheek.

-Thanks, but I'm fine.

-You always say that.

-And I always mean it.

-You know I'm here if you need to talk, right?

-I'm fine. Do you think Mel is okay?

-What do you mean?

-She's not herself.

-She's just having a good time.

-She didn't say anything?

-No, she's fine.

-Okay, I sigh. I'm getting another drink. You want one?

Lindsay's shoulders drop and she nods.

6:53AM, Sunday

The light has a tinge of red through the thin layer of skin covering my eyes; the subtle pounding is the only evidence I need that it's going to hurt to open them. A headache is there, but I'm not nauseous. Not yet, anyway. The only option at this moment is to lay completely still, push off the pain for a few more minutes. What time did I get to bed? How the hell did I get home?

After finally gaining the courage to face the day, I open my eyes. The window in front of me is unrecognizable. It's not my TV, not my couch; none of this belongs to me. This isn't my house, apartment, or whatever the hell it is. Standing up quickly was not the best course of action, no matter the amount of shock. The lamp by the front door begins to move quickly from side to side, if only in my eyes. Each hand finds the corresponding side of my head placing just enough pressure to alleviate a bit of the stress.

Damn it! How did I let this happen? Nothing in the room looks familiar. There are no photos, no mail. Where am I? My jeans are beside me on the wooden floor. The room looks old, Victorian old. The landlord slapped coat of paint on the walls, but it doesn't hide any of the age. Shit! The pain in my head won't go away. I've felt this internal hammer so many times before.

-How did I let this happen again, I mutter incoherently.

-Morning.

I don't recognize the voice and heavy footsteps enter the room from behind.

The room begins to spin as I once again turn my head faster than I should; a rumble from my stomach lets me know that I need to take it easy. Throwing up would not be good; not now. I respond with my own 'morning,' confused, looking around the room. I had to have gotten his name at some point. Remember it. Please just remember what it is. There's no escaping the situation. Morning, I say, again.

His back is to me now as he pours a glass of water in the adjoining kitchen. His broad shoulders move horizontally as he places a large bottle back into the refrigerator.

-How are you feeling this morning? He's smiling, wide and brimming.

-Rough.

-Yeah, you hit it really hard last night.

He laughs and creases form at the edge of his mouth.

-Do you even remember my name, he asks.

I'm embarrassed. The entire meeting itself is a mystery. He wasn't there earlier in the night when I helped Mel over to the table. Who lets a random stranger come home with them to crash on the couch? Be cool. You were probably in no shape to try and make it home, Ez. I look to the floor, the top of the coffee table, searching for a wallet, anything that might help me.

-Josh, he says matter-of-factly.

I laugh uncomfortably as he sits on the leather couch beside me.

-Sorry.

-It's okay. You were cute, he announces. You—are cute.

He pushes my hair back from my forehead and kisses me. I pull back quickly, my head turning from him.

-What's wrong, he asks.

Stuttered words make an appearance to no firm resolution. He looks confused, sad. I don't know how to answer. It wasn't bad—but no. This isn't who I am.

-What's wrong? You were into it last night.

Oh, fuck. What did I do? Ask him.

The lines around his mouth deepen.

-I'm sorry. I'm feeling bad, real bad.

He leans in and kisses me again. I should pull away but I don't.

-I don't usually do this. I laugh and continue: That's cliché I know.

- That's what you kept saying last night, the stranger chuckles.

-What all did we do?

He pulls back and fidgets with his thumb.

-We just made out. Is that okay?

The air drains from my mouth leaving nothing but dryness. What is there even to say at this point? It happened.

-Are you alright, he asks and places his hand on top of mine.

-Yeah, my head is just spinning and—

- And what, he probes.

I look away.

-Do you have a boyfriend?

I shake my head slightly.

-Was this your first time doing something with another guy?

Meeting his gaze proves harder than it should be as the pull of everything else in the room takes hold. I kind of nod. At least, I think I did. He wraps his fingers through mine and moves closer, turning my head softly with the palm of his hand on my cheek.

-You didn't do anything wrong. You know that, right?

I simply nod again, probably looking like an idiot in the process. The inability to form words is debilitating and embarrassing.

-You don't have to agree with me. I've been where you are, and I promise you it's okay.

-Thanks, I mumble quietly.

Josh picks up my phone from the coffee table and shows me the screen. I don't know what he is doing but enter the password to unlock the main screen.

-I'm putting my number in here. You don't have to use it, but I really hope that you do.

He reaches the small, silver rectangle to me and I examine it like a foreign object before finally taking it.

-You're freaked out right now, so I'm going to go back in my room. You can get dressed and go if you want. High Street is a block to the right out my front door. You'll know where you are from there. Do you have Uber on your phone?

Another mindless nod.

-Use that if you want. I can take you home, but I don't want you to freak out anymore than you are.

Another kiss. This time, there's little left of the feeling instructing me to move away and my hand instinctively finds his.

-Thanks, I say.

He stands up slowly, his body a shadow in the dark room, lanky, but strong. My hand drops back into my lap and he closes the door quietly behind him a moment later. The look of guilt in his eyes is one that cannot be reconciled in my heart, and I feel bad that I have made him feel the same. He's a sweet guy and hurting him was not my intention. How did this happen? How the hell did I end up going home with another guy?

Fuck.

I don't understand what is going on, the feeling it gave me when he kissed me. It was good; better than good. Amazing. There are too many emotions, all opposing one another.

Is God going to hate me for this?

What do I tell my friends? Do I need to tell them anything?

Damn it! Why did I have to let myself do this? I should have just stayed with my friends last night. My window, my walls—those should have been the familiar sights that came with the morning. With the lark. Ha!

It's not the time for a joke.

Nothing bad happened. It was a kiss, or several. Everything is fine. You can joke with yourself. Everything is fine.

There are no solid memories to assuage myself of the fear that things could have gone further. Josh's word is all that I have and relying on that—well, it's all that I have right now. What if I'd been hurt?

You're not. Stop.

Nothing is going to fix this! I knew it was coming; a blackout. I'm the one that kept going, kept drinking, and pushing my body further into the oblivion that once brought comfort. It's my own fault.

Don't think about that now.

When then?

Just get home and sleep. Sleep will help; then, these events will find some perspective. Leave here and go home. Home is safe; home is what is needed at this point.

My jeans are tight today, tighter than I remember last night; cold and stagnant. I hate them, constricted, fat, and ugly. Don't be a fucking woman. I just want to be home. Basketball shorts, in my bed; the heat caressing my winter-dry skin. Instead, I went home with a stranger.

Stupid. So fucking stupid.

Is making out all that we really did? There's no way for me to be sure, but these questions will lead to nothing but further self-destruction. What did we do?

Stop! You would know if you did more. He seemed sweet; what point would there be in lying? He looked nervous, though. He might have thought I would turn him in if I didn't remember doing something. Gah!

Fuck! FUCK, FUCK, FUCK!

Get out of here! Thinking about it is counterproductive and wasting commute time back to shelter, safety; you have his number, Ezra, if you want to talk later. Go!

My coat is on the floor; I grab it and throw my arms through the holes, fumbling and shaking, then zip it quickly and look towards the closed bedroom door. The shoebox hallway encases it in blackness, and I turn the knob to the front door. It doesn't open and the silent freak out begins to rupture from my head before my hand finds the deadbolt. With a quick crank to the right, a technicolor, somewhat familiar landscape opens before me.

The air feels better than it has ever felt on my skin before. Like freedom, like rebirth. Another overdramatic cliché this morning, but I don't care. I'm on my way home and too hungover for originality. It's stupid to even care about that, right?

My nauseous stomach is getting worse, gurgling from somewhere deep. The familiar dryness starts in my throat and even the little amount of spit my mouth can muster is not enough. I look back to the semi-rickety front porch that I have just left and puke in the bushes. My throat burns and the hot liquid finds its way out five more times before it becomes useless heaving.

God, what have I done?

What have I done?

Against what should have been better judgement, my eyes look back to see if he has come outside to watch me go, to evaluate my condition. Nothing. He probably doesn't even care. This was nothing to him.

It's nothing to me. It can't be.

I pull the back of my hand across my mouth and continue in the direction the stranger, no, Josh, had advised, only to find myself on High Street a few minutes later. Something finally seems right; each building here has a name, one that accompanies a memory. Each brick building from the turn of the century lines up next to one another like a railway, unmistakably the center of downtown.

Go right. No, left.

My contacts need cleaned; the right more so than the left. They're hazy, like my head. I run my hand through my hair and realize that it must look like I feel. It seems higher on my forehead than usual. The edges of my brown mop are usually visible at a vertical glance but not so this morning.

-I'm doing the fucking walk of shame, right now. I only sort of laugh at my whispered and ridiculous revelation.

Where are my sunglasses; I can only squint and look at the ground as I walk. Those important sunglasses are not standard evening wear. Each crack takes on a number before there are too many to continue the count, so it begins again at one hundred. Avoiding the gaze of anyone I pass becomes the second in a quickly growing series of games one can play with themselves.

There's no question what has happened to me; the mussed hair, red cheeks. I look rough; I feel rough. The phone comes from my pocket, warm and containing a message from Josh. His name brings about a smile. Should I answer? Ignore it? I start to put the phone back, but I stop and slide my finger across the screen.

Had fun last night. Sorry it freaked you out but would love to see you again.

This isn't who I am or want to be. Sweat forms and spills down my forehead and beneath my arms, cold, but refreshing. My shin feels like it is about to explode from the inside. Keep walking. You're not that far from home. Just keep going. Fight through the pain. Face the world in front of you, not just below, to make sure you are not going to run into anyone, Ez.

The streets are nearly abandoned. Well, as abandoned as they can be in a city this size. The cold breeze feels good, but it's going to be another warm day. El Niño, I think they call it, whatever that means. It's not long before this word finds its way into the search field on my phone. Something about warm oceans but interest is lost quickly.

This is the main reason that I thought it would be a good idea to go out, to enjoy myself before another cold front makes its way through. It shouldn't be this warm in January. It should be freezing. Staying home and watching television should have been enough. I should have just stayed home! It's my own fault. There's no way to deny that. Stop trying to justify what happened by blaming something else; weather is not the scapegoat in this situation. I want to go back. I want it all to not have happened.

What does he even see in me? He's way better looking than I am. Better shape. Better face. Better everything.

Did I talk to him? Did he talk to me? Why the hell can't I remember what happened? Why did he have to talk to me? I'm not someone a guy like him would talk to! Girls have had no problem ignoring me over the years, why didn't Josh?

The green sign for my street is just ahead. I can only make out a few of the letters, but it's definitely my street. You'll be home soon; only a few more minutes. Just keep walking. The pain has intensified in my leg and I think about calling a cab. Don't be a pussy, Ez. Just keep moving. Keep walking; you will be home soon.

Ignore the pain. Ignore what you've done. You'll just sleep and it will be over. You don't have to remember it. Push it out of your mind. It didn't happen. All you did was kiss him. No one will know. No one.

God, forgive me. Forgive me. Please.

I turn the corner and hit my toe on the edge of the sidewalk. Damn it! Flip flops, another bad choice. It takes a few seconds and a few steps, but a tiny red stream finds its way to the surface and falls down the side of my largest toe. I sigh and sigh again but I'm too close to home to lose my cool, to let my temper flare up right here in the middle of the city. There's no one around, but I'm not going to give in to that rage. Nothing will be accomplished by giving in to extreme emotions here on the street.

I wish Josh were here.

Where the hell did that come from? It's stupid, just stop. His hand. It felt nice to be touched like that. Human contact felt nice for once. I've never had that before; well, I have, but not like that. It always felt devoid of emotion. There has to have been some point in my life, somewhere. High School. College. No. No one has ever put their hand on me like that.

The closest I get is when Melissa gets drunk and wants to make out with me. That's pathetic; the fact I know it's pathetic makes it worse. I actually enjoy the attention that I get from someone that only wants to kiss me when she is as blackout drunk as I am.

The sound of my own laughter barrels against one building and onto another. No real reason can be determined for it but here it is. A sullen, disheveled man with a large beak finds my gaze momentarily. He pulls a cigarette to his lips and silently judges. I keep walking.

Not much longer now.

My condo comes into view, a stonemason's inferno of multicolored brick from another century rises from the concrete walkway.

-Thank God.

A small plume of smoke trickles out of the white, plastic pipe protruding from the dark shingles. Heat. Once I'm inside, everything is going to be okay. I can't wait to be warm again, as I realize my feet are freezing. This nightmare is almost over. It was one bad night. Forget it. Just forget everything that happened and sleep. Sleep for the rest of the day, as long as you need.

I reach for the doorknob and pull back slightly. What's going on? My stomach has knotted. I pull the keys from my jean pocket and slip the gold key into the lock. The heavy wood swings inward and the hall seems different. Longer, darker. Angrier.

Just go to bed. No more thinking. I shut the door, lock it, and run my hand along the brick wall as I slowly enter the living room from the entrance hall. My coat drops to the floor, swiftly with a soft thud, then my pants, a trail back to the beginning of safety. My body starts to accept the heat, but my legs feel frozen; the muscles in them refuse to unfurl, to relax. I fight the urge to let myself slide down the wall to sleep on the wooden floor.

Go to your bed. It's a few more steps. Just do it.

The stairs are steep and the darkness extends out for what could be forever had I not known the truth. A deep sigh exits, the only source I imagine is my soul, and I lift a foot, working my way towards the top. It's arduous, this journey. I limp slightly as the pain in my shin worsens. If this had been a hospital visit, I would have given the pain a six. For a moment, the only thing I can picture are the various emoticons on a pain chart. Ha! ha!

My sheets are in a heap and take the weight of my body with ease. The urge to pull the blankets over my body is fought by the lack of strength left in my arms. Sleep is the only thing left to do. I pull my second pillow to me and wrap my arms and legs around it, picturing Josh's hand on mine.

Sleep. Just sleep.

The pillow feels empty, cold, and lonely in my arms.

Sleep. Just sleep.

There are pills that can help this headache, but the distance to them is more daunting than the current pain. I'm going to regret it later if I don't. I should get some water, too. It's difficult to move. The body is a thing of wonder unless it has taken in enough alcohol to knock down a small herd of cattle.

Maybe I should just take the chance that I'll feel better later without it. Damn it; it hurts so bad! Just get up. Nah, it'll be fine.

Just get the fuck up and get some water! It will take five minutes. Stop debating. Get up. Get up. Get up! This battle of wills against mind and body is even more debilitating than actually doing it. Make a decision.

The slight roaring of the furnace fills the emptiness of the space as my journey to the bathroom commences. I avoid my reflection in the mirror, already knowing that there is no possible way I look like I have my life together. No need to reiterate it.

The mirror swings outward and my doppelganger has disappeared; one is bad enough, especially this morning. There is certainly no need for two Ezra Hayleys running around in this world.

A small orange, vaguely transparent bottle sits on the third shelf from the bottom. I hesitate before grabbing it, but my chest is tight and the yellow pill should help. My hand makes a useful cup under the flowing spigot to swallow this before I grab the Tylenol. Another cup, another gulp. Please go away, quickly.

This happens too much. I know that, and I need to cut back. I'm sure that it's going to be what kills me, and right now, that seems fine. I'm too tired to lecture myself, anymore. My hand hesitates before it can make contact with the mirrored door. I still can't face my self-destructive self. Not now.

The door to the cabinet stays open as the floor creaks out the path back to my bed and coolness has returned to the sheets. It feels just as good as I remembered from only minutes before. I lock myself back into the same fetal position around the pillow as before.

Josh.

His smile. The way his eyes fell into a squint just before that smile.

I shouldn't have done it. Why couldn't I have just stayed in last night?

Stop. Just stop. It happened. I can't take it back, so there's no use dwelling. Move on. Just move on.

How am I supposed to forget that kiss? It felt good to be kissed like that. He looked into my eyes before he closed his. Green seeing green, or some variation of my hazel.

-God, forgive me.

I'd love to see you again.

Why do I want to see him again? He could be a good friend. No, there's no use trying to be friends after that. The spark was too much. The emotions too raw, too real.

-Stop!

An unrecognizable deepness has taken over my natural speaking voice. Deep and raspy, cold and dismantled against each of the plaster walls. I really need a rug up here. Something to take away the cavernous loneliness of the space. If it's a bit homier, I might feel more like I belong.

-Go to sleep. Stop thinking.

Stop thinking. Go to sleep.

9:43AM

No!

I sit up and turn my head quickly, looking frantically from side to side. I don't remember what I was dreaming, but the sweat running from several of my orifices indicates the truth. My sleeve comes in handy as I pull it across my mouth to remove the substantial amount of drool that has accumulated there. It's only after wiping my stubble, cheek, and hand that I realize it is the button down from the night before.

Crap.

I pull it off and throw it at the wall and listen for it to hit the floor.

The sound is slight, but it's confirmation that the garment landed somewhere. It had to, right? More inconsequential questions confirm that I am nowhere near awake enough to face the day. Doping myself with the prescribed medication has lessened my irritation with—well, I guess, myself. The thumping of my pulse in my head has finally numbed and I'm doing alright.

Where is the phone?

My hand shoots under my blankets, each one separately and then under the pillow. The familiar feel of the cold steel calms the tightness in my chest, but only a bit. I trace each illuminated number reading 9:45 before throwing it to my side.

-I can still make it to church, I confirm aloud.

Do I belong there anymore? Does God want to see my face? That's a stupid thing to think; He always sees your face. He loves you no matter what; that's what you've always learned, known. Get up and go. This is what you need. It's always made you feel better when you've had problems. He's always made you feel better. Just go.

But—Josh.

Go.

I'm tired and just want to sleep. This is not how I need the world to see me right now. At my lowest, crawling out of a hole for some absolution. Who wants to be that guy? The guy that only goes to church when there is a problem.

-You have to start somewhere.

How can I be forgiven? It's not the end of the world. He *is* forgiveness.

They will see my guilt, my shame. They're gonna ask how I am and I'm going to break. I'm going to tell the world what I've done.

This isn't about them. This is about you, and God. This is about your relationship with God. Get out of bed and go to church, now!

Just go. You're awake, anyway! Get up. Get dressed. Leave.

Another ten minutes pass, and my eyes slowly open again, to the same harsh light.

There's still time to get ready and go. I throw the covers off, and the coolness of the air penetrates my open skin. The dredging to the bathroom feels eternal and damned, like walking a plank. Each piece of grooming material faces me instead of the alternative that I spared myself earlier in the morning. Do I want to face it? Or try to get ready as best I can without seeing the destruction that I have caused?

It's just me, I confirm with the closing of the cabinet. I have to start somewhere, to be brave and face myself. This is that first step. The fallout is not as bad as I had initially anticipated. Just Me. Red-eyed, messy-haired me. Not the monster I assumed would be looking back.

I wipe away the crusty mess at the corner of my eye and smile. It doesn't feel real so I let it fall away, my teeth hidden behind chapped memories of earlier this morning.

Fake it till you make it; isn't that what they say?

-You can do this, Ez.

The shower looks dingy and I commiserate with it. You need to clean that this week. Take it one room at a time and the place will look great!

The door creakily slides into place and I look around for reasons unknown even to myself. No one else is in the house. Just me. Always, just me. The water is too hot, then too cold. I'm usually better at this. Maybe I shouldn't be going out to church. If you can go out to a bar, you can go to church.

What if they smell the alcohol?

Stop thinking; there's very little need for it here, or for the most part any given situation. Overthinking is the cause of life's many problems, yet I suppose, so is under-thinking.

I need everything to stop.

There are days where I want nothing more than to be so medicated that I'm like a robot. No feelings of guilt, or pain, or even pleasure for that matter. I don't deserve the feeling of pleasure, or love; I'm sure of that. Numbness. That's the world that we live; we are told to over cope and under cope. Living one's life should not be this wildly, and completely, difficult.

The Jetstream of hot water feels good; if I were a cartoon, lines indicating smell would be wafting off of me. The scent of hard partying. The aroma of Josh's cologne, which I now realize is wavering just under my nostrils.

It gets into my head and brings his face into vivid detail once again. His lips, his eyes. His arms, his body. His chest. More details have emerged in the time since I have come home and somewhat recovered from the previous night's dalliance. My hand finds its way down my torso, then across my thigh. I think about him kissing me, fantasizing about if it had gone further. He would have kissed my neck, my chest.

-Stop, I admonish myself!

This isn't who I am.

How many times am I going to say that?

Until you believe it, Ez. Until you stick with it and believe it.

What had only been a fantasy in the back of my mind is becoming reality, a reality that I cannot foreseeably live. There's enjoyment, possibly happiness in fantasy, but I shouldn't want it.

Why shouldn't I be happy, though? Isn't that what God wants for us? Doesn't He want us to live a fulfilling life? Just because someone happens to love another guy doesn't mean that I love Jesus any less. Does it? It could be a test. A test to deny myself a pleasure I shouldn't want.

And love? That's crazy! I just met this guy. It's lust, if even that.

-No more thinking!

Think later. No, don't think again.

You have to get ready and go or you're not going to make it. Ez, buddy, you need this today. The shampoo falls from my hair, creating a puddle of white suds around my feet. Grab the body wash and the puff thing. Rinse yourself and get out.

The shower did not take the amount of time that it seemed, and I still have 30 minutes to get to church. It's been so long since I've been, and I hope the times on the services have not changed. An online search a few months ago had a few prospects, but this one stood out. Too many Saturday nights out have prevented me from actually attending a service, however. Today is going to change that. The need for fellowship and human contact is overwhelming. Maybe, it's God calling me back.

He takes our suffering and makes us whole, right?

I check myself in what has quickly become my greatest enemy and grab the mouthwash before slowly making my way to the front door. The temperature is impossible to guess, but the weather app on my phone saved me the time of pulling out a heavier coat. My coat from last night should be enough to counter the mild temperature, and it has not moved from its previous location.

Not that that would have been possible. Ha!

A quick inspection with my nostrils proves that it has not held onto the smells of the bar. It's good to go for today, I hope. A toboggan that has made its home on the small stand beside the door looks inviting. I don't need it but pull it on anyway.

The directions on my phone look simple enough to follow and I turn right at the bottom of the stairs from my front stoop, walking briskly into the wind. It has picked up, but the warmth remains. I imagine my face has turned red, however, to match my eyes. I pull the hat down further onto my forehead and walk with my head down, again counting each cement block that I cross. The British voice from the phone tells me to turn here and there.

Shouldn't be too much longer now.

The brick steeple stands above a group of leafless trees just ahead, behind a McDonalds. Almost there.

God, I need you so much right now. I know the building isn't you, but Your people are there, waiting to embrace a newcomer, I hope. I love You. So much.

Please don't let this be a bunch of judgmental people posing as Christians, bogged down by their "religion." There's no way my heart and mind can handle that this morning.

The door opens before I get the chance to reach for the handle and an older gentleman smiles and reaches for my hand.

-Welcome, son.

I reach out and grab it, squeezing tighter than I normally would have.

-Is this your first time with us, he asks, I'm sure noticing the apprehensive look on my face. Socially awkward is not a great description for it, but meeting strangers is not one of my stronger skills in life. Unless I'm drunk, of course.

-Yeah, I say, letting my gaze hit the floor.

-Well, we are happy to have you with us. I'm Pastor Rob and I'll be handling the sermon this morning. It's a tough one, but I think it will be good for a lot of people to hear.

-Thank you—sir, er—Pastor.

He laughs, continues to smile and gestures towards the pews inside the sanctuary.

-Not trying to scare you, by the way, he calls from the doorway as I move further inside.

More attendees arrive and I quickly scan the seating arrangement for someplace to sit and take it all in. A hand finds each side of my face before I run them through my hair.

Just act normal.

You are normal.

They're just people, too. They don't know what you've done. Keep it together.

The ceiling is painted with a scene from the Bible that I only vaguely recall, if at all. A smaller painting on the wall portrays a boat; Jesus walking on the shore nearby. This story, I recognize. My body drops into the back pew, at the closest edge to the stone wall.

Will they know something is wrong with me if I sit all the way back here?

No one is paying attention to you; you're another face in the crowd.

-Hey! Is it okay if I sit here?

What? There's a ton of open seating, literally almost anywhere else.

Finally, my face meets the questioning stare of a girl—woman searching my face for an answer. Her teeth nearly glow in the shadows formed from the shelves above my seat.

-Yeah, sure, I answer, stuttering a little.

What is wrong with me?

-I don't think I've seen you here before.

Her smile is warm and she looks away while running her hand down the back of her black skirt, making sure that it didn't ride up.

-I haven't. This is my first time.

-I'm Layla .

-Nice to meet you, Layla . Ezra.

-Nice to meet you, too.

She lets her fingers linger (another rhyme, ha!) in mine longer than I would assume is an appropriate duration upon first meeting. The laugh coming from my mouth doesn't feel as genuine as it probably should. Too late to adjust the sound now. Hopefully, she doesn't hear it.

She doesn't know me, so I wouldn't think she could tell the difference between true joy and an act. It's not *unreal*. Just nerves.

It's difficult to pay attention to the actual words, but I focus on her lips. Purple. Dark.

Josh.

Why can't you just let it go?

Happening this morning is not something that I could possibly be over already. I'm not a sociopath. I hope.

It's over, though. Over.

-I know this is probably a stupid question, she laughs and continues: what brings you here? Or, I guess I should say, how did you pick this church? There are tons here in the city.

My stutter seems obtrusive and obnoxious, but I'm sure it's not as bad to those around me. If so, there are no strange looks to alert me to their thoughts.

No actual words are formed in response before she continues.

-You don't have to answer, she asks genuinely. Church is a personal thing; I get that.

-It just felt right this morning; I finally say after a few minutes of us both looking towards the pulpit.

-I honestly don't know anything about you, but if you ever need to talk, I know that it can be difficult trying to start a new church.

-Thanks, I answer quickly as the pastor I'd met at the door takes his place at the front of the small congregation. Eight pews near the front of the chapel are close to capacity. I'm the slacker at the back of the class.

Should I move up?

Pay attention. You're here for a reason. And Layla 's back here with me.

-Lord, we thank you for all those in attendance today. Thank you for this day, this life, and that we have the chance to live it and glorify Your name. Lord, every day is a gift, and we thank you for that. Give me the wisdom and Your words for this sermon today. Let those who need it be touched—

God, what am I doing? What kind of person do I want to be? Who am I becoming? Please, please forgive me for what I've done.

The door softly lands in place with a thud and four or five more people straggle into the back row opposite our own.

I love You, Lord. More than anything, and I'm so sorry I let it go that far.

How did I let it go so far?

-You okay, Layla whispers and I feel her hand on mine.

My eyes are closed well into the start of the sermon before the realization comes over me. The nod of affirmation is enough for Layla to center her attention back on the pastor. His name has already slipped my mind.

-"There hath no temptation taken you but such as is common to man: but God is faithful, who will not suffer you to be tempted above that ye are able; but will with the temptation also make a way to escape, that ye may be able to bear it." Paul tells us in first Corinthians that God will always be there for us. He will not allow us to be tempted with more than we can handle, more than we can resist.

He slams his hand down and continues: We are stronger than we think we are, and it is God who loves and knows that we are more than that. We are created in His image, not to have disdain for ourselves, but to love ourselves and spread His light. His love. And His word!

He's right. There was no resistance on my part. I shouldn't have let him kiss me again. I shouldn't have let myself get drunk. It was one little word: no! But, it never crossed my lips. Body heat burnt out any common sense that should have won out. I should have stayed home.

My hand finds its way to the corner of my eye, wiping away an unexpected tear. I turn my head to face the brick and hope that no one else will notice.

He wants me to know that I have messed up. That's why I am here today.

God, please—please forgive me for this. Static flows through my fingers and my stomach is on fire.

Hot liquid finds its way into my throat and I push to swallow. Don't make a scene. Don't let it come up again.

I need to be alone.

My wrist suddenly seems bare without a watch to prove that time is still moving forward. I forgot to put it on before I left the house. Every moment feels too swift, each tick alerting the crowd to every sin that I have ever committed.

My phone lets me know that it has been an hour. The service should be over soon.

God, I'm sorry I brought this shame into your house! I'm so sorry. Pay attention. Feeling sorry for yourself is not why you came here today, Ezra. You're here for a reason. Pay attention.

-Amen, the pastor says loudly and lets his open palm slam against the wood once again.

Layla is smiling.

-He's amazing, isn't he?

-Yeah, he's great, I agree.

-Hey, are you sure that you're okay? You look a little pale.

-Yeah. I'm good. Tired. Just tired. I guess I'm not used to getting up this early on a weekend.

Probably not the best thing to say to someone that clearly makes it to service every Sunday, or something very close to this number. I used to go all the time. What happened? Where has all the time gone? So many old people say that, and now here this sentiment comes from my own mind.

The lines at the corner of Layla's mouth tighten from curves to lines. She's questioning herself as to how much I had to drink last night, now, and how late I got home. She's wondering if I went home at all. I don't know how, but somehow Layla can read my thoughts, my soul. That cute, sweet smile. She knows.

Maybe, she genuinely cares?

The bottom fourth of her arm disappears into a large, black purse, returning to the surface with a pen and piece of paper.

-Like I said, if you ever want to talk about anything, give me a call. It can seem cliquey when you first come, but the Pastor, he actually cares. He knows the love of God, and he comes from a pretty tough background. He's been there, and he overcame all that.

-What kind of background?

-You'll have to talk to him about that, but I'm sure he would love to sit down with you and discuss.

The sweat from my neck seems to work as a lubricant for my hand, my fist unclenching slightly.

-That's really nice of you, I say, scanning the number on the paper. Thank you.

-See you next Sunday, then? Her brow furrows.

-Hopefully.

I smile.

-Hopefully see you then, then, she answers back.

Layla turns to face the door, provides one last smile, and walks away, pulling each side of her coat closed before a hat completes her attempt to combat the fictional winter she will find on the front steps. The scene above my head seems to have found new life now, like each one of those men on the boat are ready to drop down into the tempest of life.

-What did you think?

The pastor places a heavy hand on my shoulder and my body jerks backwards, uncontrollably and somewhat embarrassingly. I notice that he now has more lines around his eyes and mouth than when I first encountered him before the service. It's hard to tell the age of someone with that much passion. He wipes the sweat from his forehead with the back of his hand and wipes the moisture on his black pants.

-It was great, I say, clenching my fists at my side.

-Didn't mean to scare you there, son. I just wanted to let you know that we are here if you ever need to talk. I'm not one to single you out in front of everyone. I think it sends the wrong message.

What does he mean by that? What does he think he knows about me?

-Thank you, sir. Everyone here seems friendly, very open to new people.

-Do you mind if I ask how you picked our little church?

Stop acting so nervous. He's just curious. Just answer him.

-Honestly, I found you online. You're close to my house, and the description seemed close to the church I went to back home.

-Where are you from?

-Up north. Johnstown.

-Ah, I know it. Never been though.

-You're not missing anything, I laugh.

-Thanks for stopping in today. I saw you saw with my daughter. I hope she was welcoming.

-Your daughter? Layla?

He roars loudly, and says: I know, every preacher has a daughter, and I'm no exception!

His pupils grow with this laugh and he continues: so, will I see you next week?

-Hopefully, I repeat my sentiment from earlier to Layla's father.

-Have a good week, son. I'm here most days if you have any questions. He hands me a card and pats me on the back before walking into an office at the back of the large, open room.

I turn the card in my hand for a few seconds before heading to the door and back towards my house. The blistering cold and snow that had blanketed the area a few days prior has been replaced by golden rays on my face. I shove my hands in my pocket and take deep breaths, trying to fill the pit that had formed in my stomach during the sermon.

Josh.

Dude, stop. Shut the fuck up about him! One time does not make it meaningful. He's out of your life. It was ten minutes this morning. He was sweet because you were in his house. You don't even remember the time that you spent together. He may have lied to you. He probably lied to you. It's hard to tell what happened last night. He may have drugged you to get you to come home!

Stop trying to justify your part in this. He didn't drug you. He didn't lure you home. You got drunk and went with him.

And for the first time, someone made me feel good about myself. Made me feel like I meant something. How is that wrong? How?

I wish there was someone that could just tell me definitively what to do. I want to be someone that hears God but second guess every decision that I make. These feelings. These fantasies. Too many years. Push them down, push them away. Your family will hate you. They will be disgusted.

My phone squeaks to life, moving my pocket from side to side slightly.

Hey man, you feeling ok?

It's Josh. Maybe, he really does like me. I laugh. If he still likes me after meeting blackout me, then he must be desperate.

Just text Layla . She seemed nice. See if she wants to hang out.

Text him back. Just text him. He's cool. Maybe you can be friends; it doesn't have to go further than that.

Haha yeah. Feeling a lot better than I did this morning. Sorry I acted so weird.

No worries dude. You're still cute in my book.

Whatever. You don't have to lie now that I'm sober.

No lies☺ We should get together and hang out. Maybe a drink? Coffee?

Well, I hate coffee. But I might take you up on that drink. Maybe just a few less this time around.

It's a date then!

What just happened? I can feel the skin around my mouth stretching, the warm air caressing my front teeth. He likes me?

Yeah, it's a date.

☺

What are you doing, Ez? This isn't you. It's not who you are.

Do you want to meet us for brunch at 1?

The text from Lindsay pops up as I reread the ones from Josh. I rub my eyes, contemplating my answer. The tiredness that had overtaken my morning has vanished.

Sure. Where at?

Regrets will surface tomorrow; no need to worry about it now. Just get to sleep early tonight. It'll be fine.

The Locke. See you soon!

Sounds good. See you there.

The lightened strip across the skin on my wrist reminds me once again I've neglected to wear my watch. Use your phone. It's easier, with little extra work. The screen comes to life sluggishly as the battery falls prey to its quickly approaching death.

11:43.

Is that enough time for a nap?

The subtle click from within the wood finds my ear before the door opens, the heat once again enveloping me. I, for the most part, am unnaturally cold for a guy. A tropical climate would suit me better, but for now, this is my reality.

There's plenty of time to lie down before I need to meet my friends. The chances of a timely arrival on their part are highly unlikely, so they will see me when they see me. The group will grow—it always does—and it will be fine. I climb the stairs one by one, then two by two for no apparent reason, and back to one.

It's a date.

My shoes land on the floor harshly as the comforter pulls me into its warm embrace.

It's a date.

I'm smiling. The warm feeling in my stomach. His smile. His voice. It's all there like a movie I have just walked out of, contemplating every little nuance to story and visuals.

Stop! You don't need to sound this pretentious to yourself. Save the acting for an audience. It's what they want and you'll oblige.

Don't do it. This isn't right. If you do this, there's no coming back.

There's nothing wrong with you. It's okay. He seems like a great guy. How can love be considered wrong?

Love?

This isn't love. Not this soon. It's an infatuation, and those can be destroyed if caught early enough.

It's a date.

12:41PM

You on the way yet?

My fingers roll over the screen before my eyes can fully open. It feels late, the light through the window has dimmed substantially. I'm late. No. They will be, but I'm not. Yet.

Leaving the house in just a minute. Be there in 20. Mel responds semi-promptly.

They won't. I throw the phone down beside me and rub my eyes. Why do I make these commitments I know that I am not going to want to keep, especially on a Sunday night? There's work tomorrow.

I'll stay in bed.

Does it really matter? They wouldn't think twice about bailing on me.

No, you told them you will be there. It's just down the street. Just go. Just go and relax.

I pick up my phone.

-Should I text him?

No, put your phone down. Get in the shower. Wake up and get ready. The lids of my eyes fall back into place, comforted by one another.

Get up!

You know that you are just going to fall back asleep if you don't get up now. I open my eyes again and sit on the side of the bed with my head in my hand, rubbing at each temple. The growl that comes out of my mouth sounds angry, erupting out of me into echoes against each wall. I've awakened my own inner beast just to get some lunch. I should just stay in bed. Rest for work tomorrow.

Damn. Work tomorrow. Don't think about it. It's still early today. Don't start worrying about that right now.

Water trickles against the metal roofing. Rain. Do I really want to deal with that to meet them? It doesn't sound that bad.

Still no message from Josh. Stop obsessing. He clearly likes you. Don't worry about it. I throw the phone down again and walk into the bathroom. The temperature difference from carpet to tile hits my body harder than expected. A fire burns into my shins.

-This weather is ridiculous, I mumble.

My bathroom is against the outside wall of the condo, and the small window is not insulated well. The rain begins to come down harder, pushing against the glass, hoping for some point of entry. The droplets don't even want to be out there. Argh! Sleep sounds so good right now. Pull the comforter tight around my body and forget the world for a few more hours.

The hot water reminds me that I am about to be covered in the filthy, acidic rain water. The smell of these people will mingle together into an earthy, unbearable polluted room. This is the atmosphere my friends will find and cling onto for dear life. They need to be surrounded, consumed by the fire of others.

I long for the coldness of a barren room.

The current water feels right; stay clean for as long as possible. Embrace the purity of it all.

You need to get out. Everything has to end, right?

If we could freeze a moment at will, we'd become nothing but stagnant hedonists, locked in our perfect time. Happiness doesn't work like that. The appeal of what we thought was the perfect moment will eventually fade. True perfection will come later, when our time ends. We aren't supposed to have it before then.

I step out and grab my well-worn gray towel. It's soft and the idea of replacing the comfort with newness seems ridiculous. It's familiar; it's what I need it to be, like home. The light from my cell on the back of the toilet glows against the tiled wall.

Surprise—they aren't going to be on time. Exit the group chat.

1:13.

Even when I count on them to be late, taking my time, sleep later, I still end up being the first one there.

How long? I type out quickly and throw the phone on my bed.

My head hits the pillow again.

Beep.

30 min.

Another thirty minutes, really? Tell them that you aren't going to be able to make it; this is the way out that you were looking for earlier. I'm hungry, now. No need to eat alone. There's nothing in the house to eat, nothing that I want, anyway.

The phone chirps and it takes a moment for my hand to find it wrapped up in the dark covers. Our group chat only confirms more late arrivals. The pressure in my stomach builds as I pull up the screen labeled Josh.

How's your afternoon?

More group texts. *We're almost there. Another ten minutes. I'm so sorry.*

Blah, blah.

I'm not upset. It's usual and I know that. They are good people, just not at meeting anyone at the time that they set. Neither am I, usually. That only applies to work, though. When you work for a bullshit company, it's very difficult to care.

That's a terrible attitude, but it's the truth. I could get up an hour earlier than I already do and still be the normal ten minutes late.

-Get up.

My legs find the floor once again and I reach for the jeans that I left by the bed from church. The green sweatshirt on the floor not far from the jeans looks inviting. It's practically telling me to put it on, but no, not with my friends. The Locke is no sweatshirt establishment. If it's not hip and fancy—and for some reason 200 square feet of walls that close in on us—then it's not worth 'our' time. A button down peeks out from the closet, so I grab it.

More texts.

Stairs.

Coat.

The door slams behind me, angrily. There could be an ex on the opposite side of the wall with the aggression just exhibited!

Ten minutes. See you soon, I finally type out when it's confirmed that the rest of the group is indeed on their way to the restaurant.

The walk is relatively short and the sun looks pretty, showing only slightly from behind the clouds. The rain stopped at some point between the bathroom and now, but I could not tell you when exactly it had. Still, like this morning, there is hardly anyone out. It seems like today would be inviting to some crowds. I would imagine an April day had I not known the truth.

Sometimes you don't want to face what you know won't last, though. The warmth will fade back into snowfall, or worse, bitter, arctic coldness.

Don't think of that now. Enjoy the sun while you have it beating down on you.

Not bad, yours? Josh answers his own text. Another pops up. *Sorry, I read that wrong and thought you answered me. I promise I'm not weird ☺.*

I should answer him, but it seems unreal. A giddiness of sorts rises in my chest; it feels like crushing on someone in high school. Do we ever really lose the feeling of excitement when we meet someone and click? Calm it down, man. We literally just met today.

Is it wrong to be this happy about meeting someone?

It's too fast. It won't amount to anything, you know that, Ez.

Melissa throws up her arm from the opposite end of the block, stopping in front of a concrete building. I assume it's the restaurant, but the sun is shining too bright to read the sign above her. Lindsay is not far behind and she looks amazing. I don't think that I've ever actually seen her look bad. Her party girl attire and flirty personality juxtapose against her natural ability to remain in control of herself. It is, however, very entertaining when she does let loose and truths start to pour out.

We are a lot alike in that aspect. Don't tell me a secret that you want me to keep when I am drinking. Well, I shouldn't say that. I can keep a secret, but it needs to be one that I deem is worthy of being a secret. I probably fancy myself as something more than that in, a sort of gatekeeper who decides if your secret should be shared or stored away for safekeeping. The sad thing is, I can see my own flaws, but I don't—or won't—fix them.

Laziness, first and foremost. Not sure where it comes from, but sitting around, daydreaming could be a career—if it paid. Ha!

I stop and lean against the side of the building before the girls can see me.

Perhaps lazy isn't the right word, or the right feeling. I'm burnt out; I'm tired of the act of living out this life. It's become exhausting. Repetitive. It's become boring and sad. Lethargic might be the better term to describe the condition. How did I even get here?

I was young.

I'm still young.

Not young enough to matter anymore. College, that's when people notice your talents, your skills. After that, it's downhill. You fade into obscurity. I had dreams for myself once but those have buried themselves; or, I buried them deep beneath multiple disappointments. I've settled into my medium-paying job that imprisons you by paying more than their competitors.

Now, I'm stuck. Another drone, dying one day at a time and losing count of how much longer I should have left.

-Ez, dude, what are you doing over here?

Nick's bulky frame casts a shadow over the minimal amount of sun that has decided to show its face, even here to the side of the building.

-Staying out of the wind for a minute.

-I thought I saw you duck back here. Everything okay?

-Yeah, fine.

-Okay. Come on, everyone is here.

My breath is more laborious than I would have imagined in pushing myself away from the brick wall that had become my support.

-How you doing? I ask.

-I'm good, man.

-Where were you last night? I thought you were going to come out with us.

-Too cold.

-Pussy, I mumble.

-Call me a pussy all you want, but I'm sure I feel a hell of a lot better than you do today. They said you disappeared.

I try to laugh it off before responding:

-I feel great, actually!

-Alright, then. I stand corrected.

He smacks me on the back heavily as I move in front of him to meet the group that is still standing outside the stained glass door.

-Hey guys, I say.

-Where did you end up last night? Lindsay asks without hesitation.

I, however, do hesitate.

-Oh, you know me. I wandered off and ended up back at the condo.

There's a chuckle, though from who, I cannot be certain. Lindsay goes on to say that this sounds like me and reaches for the door handle.

My hand finds the handle just before hers and I gesture for her to move inside once the door has been opened.

The smells inside are strong, yet unrecognizable, and the rumbling in my stomach is a mix of nausea and hunger. Near exhaustion finds its way into my head and my body. My nap was clearly not enough to sustain the trip out. I need to be able to make a run for the bathroom should this sick feeling continue to grow inside of me.

-How do you feel today? I ask Lindsay, who has found a seat next to me.

-I'm good, she answers and begins some separate conversation with Melissa no doubt scolding her for how drunk she had decided to get the night before.

Lindsay is a wonderful person; I won't debate you on that, but she has a standard that she feels needs to be met so as not to be part of one of her makeshift counseling sessions. She probably should have been a psychiatrist but that's not what interests her. At least, not in the professional sense of the word. She wants to be a teacher. Part of me thinks that she will make a terrific teacher, but the other thinks that she will be too hard on the students. It's so easy to undermine a child's self-confidence, especially when your version of perfection will never be met.

That's a lesson everyone learns in their own time. We never quite live up to others expectations.

-What are you thinking about, Melissa asks as she places her hand on my shoulder and squeezes.

It's been a few minutes and my attention had drifted from the rest of the group. Nothing, I answer and issue a statement about the failing health of my current stomach. She laughs and continues to make her way around the long table, saying hello to each new member of the group that arrives in succession over the next twenty minutes.

I realize now that I am simply hungry—starving, but who knows how long it will be before we are "allowed" to order.

The group continues to grow; we're at eleven now. A few faces remain unrecognizable, but that's the facts of how things go within this group. I am only one small part, one minute piece of the puzzle that makes a day—a night—out memorable for our host, our Clarissa Dalloway.

-What are you laughing about, Lindsay turns to me suddenly.

-Nothing, sorry. I'm just tired.

-You're a mess.

-Yup.

It's another joke that would not have gone over as well as it had in my head. Perhaps one day I can retreat in my head and live into a place where I require only my own understanding. A lonely, subdued place that I would never have to explain my jokes or experience the stares that accompany such an attempt at comedy.

Stop feeling sorry for yourself. There's really no need. I keep myself tuned into pop culture, and I can make a sarcastic joke with the best of them, but it's these jokes I find so clever that they do not.

Who cares what they think? Be yourself.

Ha! I'm an outsider.

Considering yourself an outsider is the hallmark of any teenager, but at what point should that change? I, for one, feel like it can follow you for a lifetime. As a child you believe your parents have it all together, and you never think that they could be just as scared as you.

I'm not even sure at what point I realized that you never really have your grip on what it means to be an adult. We all just fumble around and hope that we don't hurt anyone in the process, clinging to a group of likeminded individuals. Just like middle school. Just like high school.

But, the alienation that comes with that can be brutal. It can decimate any fondness that one might hold for themselves. I've spent even more time building the illusion that I am an insider, working desperately to attain relationships that I'm not sure I want in the first place.

It's taken nearly a decade—not sure if it takes that long for everyone—but, I've made some peace with the fact that every phase in life is the same. Cyclical and heartbreaking. High school—maybe middle—is where the mind games start. Someone is always trying to outdo and destroy you in some fucked up way. It makes no sense, but there is always someone that wants to take you down.

Take you down?

I'm not sure if that is the best way to put it, but it's vaguely true. Someone always thinks they are better and will go out of their way to prove it. The sheer fact that kids are killing themselves should teach us a lesson, but it doesn't. We superficially sympathize, smile in comfort, and move on with our lives. It's a new form of bitter humanism that even I have come to participate.

-I'll have a whiskey and ginger ale, I tell the brunette waitress as she finds her way within earshot. It's funny, or ironic, or whatever—that she cannot even purchase the drink that she is about to bring me. She sits a glass of water down and I thank her.

-What are you getting, Nick asks from my right side.

-Did you not hear me order?

-To eat, asshole, he jibes me for my remark.

-I don't know. Think it's rich people portions?

-What, Nick laughs.

-You know, super expensive but not enough to fill you up.

-Ah.

-Have you been here before?

-No, but look at this place. My guess is yes.

For the first time since we sat down, I take my eyes from the menu and take in the full extent of the room. I've finally let myself become comfortable in the space, surrounded by people within our group.

The room is fairly impressive. Exposed brick. Glass shelves with liquor bottles separating two rooms, the bar and the dining room. The dull light of the enormous chandelier casts a perfect glow to give the effect that it is always dusk inside the small building.

My drink arrives and I take a sip, letting the warmth of the bourbon warm my chest and the ginger taste layer my taste buds. The warmth never gets old. A second sip goes down easier and I look over the menu again. I grab the rocks glass another moment later and finish the drink. The waitress does not miss this and asks if she can bring another. I nod and she moves away quickly.

-What are you getting, Nick asks again without looking up from the brown parchment—an upscale touch—in front of him. I can only see his blonde, shaved scalp move up and down.

-The steak, maybe?

-Glad you're okay, Lindsay says from behind me as her arms meet in front of my neck.

-What do you mean?

The stealth in finding herself behind me is impressive. I'm not sure if there is too much noise in the room or if I really am that unaware.

-You disappeared, she answered.

-I always disappear.

-That's true. Where did you go?

I pause, pondering the truth. Josh. His lips. His kiss.

-I just staggered home, I finally answer.

-You could have had a good time if you'd stayed.

-What do you mean?

She motions with only her eyes towards Melissa.

-She was all over you last night.

-She was drunk. She's always like that when she's drunk.

-She said you were cute.

Heat travels into my cheeks, and I imagine that they have turned red, causing my face to inadvertently turn away from Lindsay into a shadow. The waitress puts a drink in front of me and I grab for the glass quickly; another entrance missed in all the thoughts. A long gulp draws the heat from my cheeks back to my chest.

-She was drunk, Lindsay. We all were.

-Okay, she says and rolls her eyes. But, she continues, I'm going to keep my eyes on both of you, and if I see more, I *will* find a way to get you together.

The chuckle that erupts from my mouth is insincere, but she doesn't seem to notice as she moves back to her chair on the other side of Mel. What is Lindsay thinking right now?

Where did this come from? We have all been friends for years and suddenly she wants to set me up with someone that has been here with us forever?

Was it a test? Did I do something last night that made her question me?

I remember dancing to some rap song in the middle of the group, spilling some beer, and walking back to the bar for napkins and another round of shots. That's it—it's the last thing that I remember.

More gulps quickly diminish the liquid, leaving just enough in the bottom to hold me over if the waitress does not notice immediately that I am in need of another. My head turns slowly, and I wonder if anyone realizes how long I have let myself zone out. It's almost an astral projection from my body to a place where I can't recall the details.

My body—of course—was left behind as a placeholder should anyone need to know that I am safe. Other than this physical being, I am gone, lost in the secret passages of my memories, searching desperately for nights forgotten. What have I done on these other nights that I have run off and don't remember? Why do I keep letting it happen? For all the danger, there is little regard for my own life. And, maybe that's the way that I want it.

-Another drink, sir?

This is not the same voice to which I have grown accustomed this afternoon. A young man, probably 21 or 22, smiles down at me. I can feel my cheeks turn red again.

-Yes, please, I stutter out like a sputtering engine.

-Whiskey and ginger?

-Yeah.

-I'll be right back with that.

-Thanks.

-You have fun last night? Melissa has apparently been trying to get my attention for the last few minutes.

-Are you alright, she asks.

-Yeah, sorry. Zoned, I guess. And yea, last night was great.

-How are you feeling?

-I'm fine. You?

-I feel like I got hit by a bus.

-You look good, though.

-Shut up. She leans over, and for a minute, I think that she is going to kiss me on the cheek. Instead, she whispers in my ear: let's get shots.

I laugh and say what, letting her know that I think the idea is crazy. At least, I hope she could hear all that in my tone.

-Come on, she whispers. Let's get shots.

-At the bar?

-Where else?

I smile and look around the table. No one is paying attention. The preferential treatment of strangers, well strangers to me, is becoming habit at this brunch, and calling it that has become somewhat of a stretch. The meal technically has just turned into lunch since everyone was so late. Though somewhat odd for me, I have no desire to be the center of attention today. A low profile provokes little to no questions. No lies.

I don't want to lie, but last night is something I am not willing to talk about. I'm not sure there's a time in my life that I will ever want to talk about it.

-You know I'm not one to turn down liquor.

-Alright, then.

She grabs my hand and pulls me out of my seat. The concrete bar stretches fifteen feet before it adjusts 90 degrees. A small crowd has formed to the larger end, a wedding party of some kind. I don't know if they have just gotten married or some kind of after-rehearsal get together.

Mel pushes her long, bleached-out hair behind her ear and orders something. I can't hear her, and I don't think the guy at the bar can either. She holds up two fingers and the blonde bartender nods and grabs a shaker.

-What did you order, I ask.

-You'll see when it gets here, she smiles.

Mel grabs the shot glasses before they can even reach the cement and hands me one.

-Bottoms up, bitch, she yells laughing.

She might still be a little drunk from last night. I take the shot without smelling it. There's no use in bringing up the nausea that I have kept at bay for most of the day, except for an instance here and there.

-Tequila?

-What else, she answers.

I put the glass back on the table and see her hold up two fingers. No one else is at the bar now, so I'm not sure why we are still standing here. The wedding party filed out after a round of shots. Perhaps it is a bar crawl. There was little evidence to support the wedding party theory, though that was the choice in my head. I pray there is no gum on the bottom of the stool as I pull it out and sit down, letting my hands fall on top of the bar.

-What are you doing, she asks?

-I just have this feeling that we are going to be here for a bit. Am I wrong? I wink.

What did I do that for? Who am I?

-Did you just wink at me, she asks, laughing.

-Apparently, I make it sound as sarcastic as possible.

-You think you can handle another shot? You seem to be a mess already.

-Mhmm.

Two more glasses of silver tequila arrive.

-You sure, she says and holds a glass out to me.

-Are you kidding?

My fingers encompass the small glass and I shoot the 1800 before she can reach back to grab her own.

-Two more please, I say loudly to the bartender, standing back smiling like a model. He runs his hand through his surfer boy hair and grabs the bottle. He holds it out to us, his arms flexing tight against his white button down shirt.

-Should I just give you the bottle, he jokes.

We exchange glances, only semi-seriously, and I shake my head slowly. I must look like an idiot, so I turn away and meet my own eyes in the mirror behind the bar. God, I look like a fat ass. I push my chin out to get rid of the second one that has now formed just underneath the first. When did this happen to me? When did I get to be this whale?

-Ezra, Mel yells.

-What?

Our foreheads nearly meet and her eyes are dilated. She looks down and pulls back slightly.

-What the hell are you doing? Drunk?

-You wish.

We slap our glasses together and guzzle the liquor. The taste no longer has an effect, and it's gone in just a moment.

-Another, the bartender asks.

Silence.

-We should probably get back to the group, I say to Melissa.

-He's right, we should probably get back to the group, she says to the bartender, laughing. You're cute, you know that?

I look up quickly from the bill that has just been placed in front of me and stare at Melissa intently. Did she really just say that to him? In the middle of the day? On a Sunday?

Sunday Funday, I guess.

I just shake my head and pull my card from my wallet, placing it in the middle of the leather case holding the receipt.

-Thanks, surfer boy says.

-Want my number?

My hand finds its way around Mel's arm and I usher her in front of me towards the table.

-Sorry about that, I say.

-No worries, he smiles.

-Well, do you, she says, looking over my shoulder.

-I really appreciate the offer, but—

-You're gay, she doesn't let him finish.

He laughs and nods.

-Do you want his number?

Her head gestures right into my cheek. I rub my cheek and apologize to the bartender.

-Doesn't sound like he's offering it, the bartender counters.

My feet stop and Mel pushes my body back slightly. He smiles at me as he grabs the two glasses we had just emptied. The blood rushes to my cheeks and I grab her by the arm again lightly, gesturing towards the table.

-What the hell was that about, I ask when we turn the corner at the liquor shelves.

-It was just a joke!

-Okay, whatever.

-Are you mad?

-No.

-It's just a joke!

She punches my arm and I start to laugh, reluctantly.

-Where have you two been, Lindsay asks loudly when she looks up and sees us.

-Uh, the bathroom, Mel responds. She then looks at me and busts out laughing.

-Is she drunk?

-Well, not yet, but I think that she will be in ten minutes or so, I answer.

-You two are a mess!

-Nah. That's just crazy talk!

Our seats have remained open in the interim, so we find our way back to them quickly. The waiter approaches me and asks if I'd like another drink. The familiar feeling from last night that is forming in my head lets me know that I had better switch to water for a bit.

He nods and walks away. Everyone is still looking at their menus as I gaze around the table. No one has ordered yet; I'd forgotten if we had or not. The water coats my throat and brings a cool relief that had been missing from my night. What did I want before going to the bar? What sounds good? My appetite is gone. That's not good, I imagine, so I will order something anyway. Take the edge off the whiskey that I can now feel in my head. The laughter I didn't even realize was coming from me brought stares from the table.

-Sorry, just thought of something in my head, I say louder than I intend.

-What did you guys do at the bar, Nick asks.

-The bathroom, Lindsay chimes in, laughing at herself.

-Just some tequila, I finally whisper.

He laughs and says: You two are pretty much made for each other.

-I guess.

Nick slaps me on the back.

-You better get on that!

I laugh.

-Speaking of, Nick lowers his voice and averts his gaze from me to the space above my head.

My head nearly collides with Mel's as I quickly turn.

-Where are we going after this, she asks?

-What?

-Where are we going?

-You want to go out again, Mel, Nick asks slightly, if unreasonably, surprised at this revelation.

-Hell yeah!

-Well, count me out! You know that I will feel like garbage in the morning and I would hate to blame you two, he laughs.

-Then drink, brah, Melissa yells. You'll forget that you have to be up early in no time.

-That won't do me any good tomorrow when I have to work. You two have fun!

-So—where are we going, she continues, squeezing each shoulder simultaneously.

-Do you really think that's a good idea? I have work tomorrow, too.

-Come on, can't you call off?

-You know I can't do that. How else will I pay for these nights out with you?

-We definitely don't want to have to stop doing that.

Her smile turns mischievous as only one corner of her mouth lifts. Mel's pupils come together in a squint and she looks away, laughing suddenly.

-What in the hell are you laughing at?

-I honestly have no idea.

I begin to laugh and notice that people from other tables are beginning to look our way. With a lowered voice and head, I motion the way of the stares.

-Fuck ‘em, she says and I push my chair backwards quickly.

-Where are you going, she asks.

-To the bathroom.

The rooms spins slightly, but my feet move away from the table to the back of the room. I’m not exactly sure where the bathroom is, but this is a nice place, and I don’t want to look as drunk as I’m beginning to feel on a Sunday afternoon. The bartender’s white smile catches my eye as I glance in the direction of the bar before quickly returning my vision to a hallway that I can only assume holds the restroom.

Luckily, or predictably, or I dunno, I am right, and the door opens to reveal a man in a suit. He’s tall; a head above myself. Must be 6’6” at least. I used to wish that I was taller, but now I find that I’m happy with myself. At least, in that regard.

There is no lock on the door, so I head for the first stall. The lid is down and I move on. I don’t want to touch it. Another stall. This lid is down also, so I use the bottom of my boat shoe to lift it. The thought of touching the bottom of the seat makes me gag a little even though I would immediately wash my hands. I used to be crazier about germs, but that has somewhat subsided as my twenties begin to fizzle out.

A smile forms on my face at the old adage, "God made dirt, dirt won't hurt." A part of my brain registers the sound of the door opening and slowly closing, but most of it is completely focused on the stream of piss that I unleash into the bowl below.

Clear. Well-hydrated.

My laugh echoes inside the small stall as I zip up and unlock the black, granite-patterned door.

The water from the spigot is cold momentarily, then too hot. It takes a moment of adjusting to get it just right and then my hands find a home under the stream of water.

A flush. A click. Footsteps.

-You know, you never did answer my question about that number.

The nervousness that had risen inside me at his smile returned quickly. Who came up with the saying about dirt?

What? Answer him.

-What do you mean, I ask, semi-jokingly.

-Your friend was going to give me your phone number, but I never did get it.

I focus on washing my hands as the bartender approaches the sink next to mine. He places his own hands under the water and looks at me in the mirror. I can feel my cheeks flushing.

-What's your name?

-Ezra.

-I'm Frankie.

-Hey, man.

-Just let me get your number.

-I don't think that's a good idea.

-Why not?

-I'm not—

-You're not what? Gay?

Frankie grabs a handful of paper towels as I shut off the stream of water. He purposely flexes his biceps and chest while drying his hands. He moves closer, leaning in close and throws the wad of paper towels away behind me. I only slightly turn my head away and he whispers in my ear.

-What's the worst that could happen? Let me get your number.

The distance between us grows with a quick motion of my feet.

-How about this? I give you my number, and you can use it if you want.

No words come to mind. I simply nod and pull my phone from my pocket, handing it to him. Whether on purpose or not, the muscles beneath his white dress shirt pulse, particularly right above the cuff that has been pushed to the top of his forearm. He hands the phone back and leaves the room. The screen is still open to the new number. Frankie B. There's no indication what the B stands for, and I guess there wouldn't be. Maybe, it's something he wants me to find out. Maybe not.

I need to get out of here or my friends are going to think that I am shitting.

Only Mel looks at me when I return, asking where the hell I've been. Some story about my pants getting wet spewed from my mouth and she seemed to accept this, only half-heartedly looking down to see if I was telling the truth. She won't remember tomorrow. The glazed look that she gets when drunk has already taken over and she just nods.

-So, where are we going after this, she persists.

-Where do you want to go?

-What do you guys think? She asks the rest of the group who look immediately and uncomfortably due to the volume of her question.

-Here. Drink this.

I hand her a glass of water.

-I don't want that!

-Yeah, but you want to be able to go out don't you? You are going to get too drunk and have to go home soon if you don't.

She hesitates and her eyelids pull together tightly. I don't know what decision she is going to make; I can't read her tonight. Mel takes the glass of water and chugs it. I push mine towards her and she chugs that too.

-Feel any better?

-What's your version of better? If you mean sober, no, but on the way there.

She flashes her fake, unimpressed smile that I know so well. Don't be like this.

She continues: Let's go. Her chair nearly falls over as she finds her footing near the table, which shakes. More stares, though thankfully, of concern and not anger.

Is this how they see me when I drink?

Mel pulls the strap of her purse over her shoulder.

-We haven't even paid yet, I insist.

-Yeah, while you were taking forever in the bathroom, I paid for you.

-That's crazy! How much do I owe you?

-Don't worry about it.

-You don't have to do that.

-Stop! Just get me back at the bar, okay?

I hesitate, then say fine.

5:35PM

Things have spiraled quickly into the normalcy that I am reluctant to admit about, and to, myself. The room is literally moving ever so slightly as I pull on my coat and walk to the door at the front of the restaurant. I carefully pat my phone, thinking about the encounter in the bathroom.

What's going on today? None of this makes sense. No one has paid any attention before.

Maybe I didn't notice? Maybe.

He's going to be gay. Is that what you want? A fag for a son.

My father's voice suddenly booms through my head. A sound so loud, so clear, so unwarranted that I stop walking.

Is that what you want?

Mel runs into my back.

-What's wrong with you, she bellows, and her forehead bounces off my shoulder.

-Sorry.

-Look, I got makeup on your shirt. She begins to wipe it away.

-Leave it, it'll come out in the wash.

-You sure?

I don't answer; my feet began shuffling forward again. Mel walks around me. The door feels heavier against my arms then before, before the drinks started changing everything, and I look back to the bartender as he hands another guy a drink. How can I do this? How can I destroy my family with this?

-Okay, then, Mel mutters.

You haven't done anything with him; he gave you his number. Absolutely nothing has to come from that or go any further.

Stop it now; forget it all. Just drink, push everything away. If you don't even know your name, you can't remember anyone else. Shove it out of your mind, Ez. A deep breath and a fake smile proceed me as I fall into step beside Melissa on the sidewalk.

-Where are we going, I ask.

She makes a series of noises that I can only guess are taking the place of Uh, but it's all slurred severely. This is like a car wreck that you can see coming but don't know how to stop.

This may not be the best idea, but I am tired of thinking today. There's been too much of it. I check my phone while Mel is trying to make up her mind. A text from Josh.

How's your night, cutie?

Josh.

I move to answer but my hand lets it drop into my pocket first.

It's warm, still.

Am I that drunk, or is it really this warm? I look around to see that the snow has already begun melting. Life in the Midwest. It's a shit show.

There was something on the news, I think.

Or maybe it was the app on my phone.

Something about a warm front that would come through and it will get to be sixty-five tomorrow. Fifty-four today and sixty-five tomorrow. I really should be used to this by now. A complaint now would be nothing but crazy talk. It's still winter, and we are going to get a nice day.

-Can you believe how warm it is, Mel asks, and I laugh.

This happens more often than not, this random reading of one another's mind. Hm. Maybe, we are meant to be together. Ha.

-So, where are we going, I implore.

-Do you think someone has a patio open?

-No Mel, I say sarcastically. It was 30 degrees colder two days ago. It could end up being that again in two more hours.

-True. Let's do The Ale Locker.

-Looking for yourself a bro?

-No, are you? She smiles and pushes me slightly.

-Shut. Up.

I'm not sure what's happening, but Mel gets quiet. Is it her or me? The warm air vaguely reminds me of an ocean breeze. I unzip my jacket and feel the drops of sweat inside my shirt. Damn it, I'm going to be pitting all over the place. Super attractive. I look down and notice my gut. I know in the whole scheme of things that I'm not fat, but nothing fits. I'm not remotely fat in the traditional sense, but I'm at my biggest. I hate it.

He's gonna be gay.

What did Mel mean by "am I" looking for a bro? Does she know something that I don't know? Did something happen the other night that she remembers and I don't? Stop examining everything she says. She's drunk as fuck!

-Where are you guys going? Nick yells as he finally exits the door behind us, some one hundred feet behind.

-Ale Locker, Mel screams.

-Come on guys, it's Sunday! We have work tomorrow.

-Just for a little bit, I say.

-Yeah, just for a little bit, Mel nods.

The hopeful look on her face reminds me of a child. A child who's gone astray and lost their mind. One who needs to be reined in, one who needs remediated into proper society. I wish I could be that person; the person that could control themselves and protect others.

I can't. Probably, won't. I would say that is more accurate. I don't want the responsibility of being an adult, but I am an adult. There's no way to change that. I don't know if it's really because I'm a man or because I feel like I was an adult years ago.

I didn't take risks, didn't live for me, or maybe I did. I don't know anymore. Back then, whenever it was, there was the common knowledge that I was a good person. I literally gave everything that I had to give to those around me.

It's so easy to walk away from me, though. It's so damn simple. I sometimes wish that I could be like that, too. I wish that I could walk away from the people that I know don't care, but this need for affection is overwhelming.

Is that wrong?

So many people would say so. There are quotes about giving no fucks and such, but not being liked bothers me. I try harder than anyone should have to try. In an interview about my life, this would be my greatest fault and deepest regret.

A whoosh of air hits me in the face as we open the door to the Ale Locker. It looks huge, the crowd smaller than what would normally be there at the beginning of the weekend. The brick floor and walls extend back to the kitchen and bathrooms near the back of the extensive room. Long, heavy beams run parallel to one another from front to back.

-What do you want? Mel screams into my ear.

-Huh?

-What do you want? First round is on me.

-An hour. One hour, Nick says from the doorway behind me.

-That's more than I expected, dude, I laugh.

-What the hell do you two want?

-Bud Light, Nick does not hesitate.

I see her turn and whisper something to a woman with cropped hair and tattoos running the length of both arms.

-Something tells me that she is not ordering that, I repeat my thoughts close to Nick's ear.

-Yeah, I figured, but for my own conscience, I had to try. He sniggers.

Mel grabs a tray from the bar and stumbles back to the table we have found. Four large glasses, garnished with a lemon, rock back and forth precariously.

-Long Islands! Woo!

-Ok, then, I say and grab a glass for Nick and myself.

-What are you trying to do to us? Nick probes jovially.

-It's Long Island night, and I'm on a budget, bitches. Drink up!

The coolness of the glass feels pleasant enough and I leave it there a moment longer than I normally would. I can't imagine that it's a good sign the alcohol has lost most of its sting. This is how it usually begins. Then I'm gone. I come to, and I feel guilty. Stopping has no longer become an option. I still should. But, why can't I?

I pull my phone from my pocket. Messages from Josh.

Having a good night?

Yeah. What are you up to?

Just got to Revolver.

The gay bar?

Stupid. Why would I ask him that? It's ignorant and just the kind of the thing that would push him away. But, don't I want to get rid of him?

Yeah. His reply is simple, and I hope he forgives my idiocy.

How is it?

Crowded, but looks like it's going to be a good time. You should meet me for a few drinks.

I'm with friends now, but if we get done early, I'll definitely try.

I wasn't sure myself if this was a lie.

How long are you going to be there, I continue typing.

Probably for the rest of the night. Closing it down! Haha!

I'll see what I can do then. ☺

Hope to see you soon, then.

I start to put my phone away and think of Frankie. His smile. His arms.

Do you want your son to grow up to be a fag? Your son. I know that his spite was fueled by the endless supply of beer. Never look up gay porn on your parent's computer, even out of curiosity. You can try and explain it away, but they will always question.

Your son.

-You okay? Nicks asks.

-Yeah, fine. What's up?

-You disappeared there for a minute.

-I think I'm drunk.

-Of course.

It's a joke. I know that it's a joke, but I am tired tonight and it feels deeper, more personal. I just want to go to bed. I should go home.

Why don't I just go home?

They are all used to me being drunk. It's not fun anymore. But, it is fun. I feel like I've done this all backwards. I never took the time to be crazy when I was younger. I wanted to be perfect. That was stupid because it was never going to happen. Perfect is such an irresponsible word. No one here can ever expect that, yet we do. We all want perfection.

Your son. Fag. Gay.

Did you finish up at work? I rattle off a message to Frankie.

-Who are you texting, Mel asks.

-No one.

-Come on, who are you texting?

-My mom texted me.

-Oh. Well, show me then. Seems kinda late for her, right?

-Your drink is gone.

She looks down quickly, fearful, like I told her a snake was about to crawl across her feet. The look on her face scares me a little but also bemuses me. Her mouth drops and her eyes dilate. Mel's horrified, horrified that she would let her drink fall so low without realizing it.

Is this how I am?

-I'll be back, she murmurs and heads back to the long beam of wood to the right of the room. The bar is thin, modern. Seems very ineffective, but I'm no architect or interior designer. I'm sure it's fine, just don't wave your arms around when you're drunk.

-Do you think she should be having another, Nick asks.

-Let her have one more, and then I'll walk her home.

-She wants you, you know?

-What? Fuck off, dude, she does not.

-I'm serious! Why do you think she always tries to kiss you when she is trashed? Do you really not see it?

-I guess not. No one really pays much attention to me.

-First off, that's bull and you know it. We all know when you're drunk, he smiles and continues: you just don't pay attention, buddy. She's been hitting on you all night.

My chin finds my shoulder in an attempt to catch Mel, I don't even know, looking my way, smiling. This is more confusing than it should be. She's drunk. You do, and feel, things when you're drunk that you wouldn't normally do otherwise.

-You walk her home, I blurt out suddenly, my eyes averted to a television showing a basketball game. It's of no concern to me who is playing at the moment.

My hands and legs tremor against one another in different directions, like tectonic plates.

-What? Nick waits till I face him, the lines in his forehead sinking deeper than normal.

-You walk her home. If she's been hitting on me all night, like you say, she's going to ask me to stay.

-Okay? His voice heightens in pitch at the end.

-I'm not going to take advantage of the situation, man. I don't want her to think I'm an asshole either. Will you please just make sure that she gets home alright?

-Yeah, of course, dude.

Nick takes a swig of his Long Island, forgoing the straw that lands against his cheek, and continues: You're right; it's probably best.

Yeah, just changing and heading out. You out?

-Dude, who are you texting?

-I told you, it's my mom.

-Your mom doesn't make you smile like that, Norman Bates.

-Be right back, I have to pee.

-Ez, come on, who are you talking to? What's wrong with you tonight?

-I'll be right back.

-Where are you going, Mel asks as I walk behind her towards the back of the room.

-Just to the bathroom. I'll be right back.

-What do you want to drink?

-Nothing, we are going to head out after this.

-Head out? To where?

-Home. I'm exhausted, and I know that you have to be, too!

-You're probably right.

-For once—I know I'm right, I laugh and pull her close.

I continue: You are going to thank me for this in the morning when your head doesn't explode.

-I love you, she says and kisses my neck.

-You're drunk.

I push her away slowly, trying not to meet her eyes. I can't disappoint someone else, not like this. Not tonight.

How have I not noticed this before? No one ever pays attention to me?

Maybe, I'm more sober than usual. More observant. It's a stretch, but it happens.

Is it wrong to be a little selfish?

I'm always selfish. I want to hang out with someone, someone who is going to focus on me. You have that right here, I'm reminded from somewhere in the back of my mind. I don't want that.

I should want that.

Do you want a fag for a son?

Shut up! I shake my head violently. The voice is getting clearer, and the slurs more evident. Even in my head he's drunk. He could be standing beside me, but I'm too afraid to look. What if it's real?

The crowd seems to have thinned some upon my return from the bathroom; I can see Nick's shaved head above the rest of the crowd. The line was longer than I cared for, but it gave me time to come back down some from the spinning room at the previous restaurant.

-You sure you're alright, man, Nick asks nearly as soon as I rejoin them in a back corner.

-Yeah, yeah.

Melissa is swaying back and forth, her Mason jar half empty. I'm not sure what it holds, but something fruity would be a good guess. The lights from a nearby DJ illuminate her face in assorted colors, and she has not opened her eyes to know that I have made it back safely.

-You're headed home, too, right? Nick asks.

-Yeah, let me settle up and then I'll meet you outside.

-Alright.

It occurs to me that I don't remember opening a tab, but I must have. Mel must have had my card. I pull my phone from my pocket once they are out of sight.

I answer: *yeah, just finishing up at The Ale Locker.*

I smile at the girl in tiny black shorts behind the bar and give her my name. She turns and looks intently into the small screen in front of her. The look on her face, seen via the mirror just above the various liquor bottles, shows concern. Her messy hair, somewhere between a bun and ponytail, disappears first as she pivots to meet my gaze, letting her ear fall a little closer to me this time. After an inquiry about my name for a second time, she turns and begins poking at the computer screen. Her head shakes slowly.

-Are you sure you opened a tab, she asks inquisitively.

Before my head finishes a full nod, the familiar hardness of plastic in my pocket jogs my memory.

How did I forget not starting a tab?

My laugh seems contrived upon showing her my mistake, but she graciously grins and pulls a pink sweatband back into place on her arm. The smile is forced, just as my laugh had been a moment earlier, but I don't blame her. It was stupid and wasted both our time. No tab. When was the last time that I had no tab to deal with at the end of the night?

It's been years. In fact, I'm still paying towards some of those college tabs in the form of old credit cards. A yawn is quickly consumed into the technical workings of some Dubstep song, and tonight feels different. I'm tired, but I'm not blackout drunk.

I pull out my phone. Two messages.

Josh: How's your night? Doing anything fun?

Frankie: Revolver. See you in a few ;)

Go home, Ezra. There is no reason for you to continue on with this night. It's over, you're an adult, so be one for a change. Your friends are leaving, and you barely know these guys. It's wrong. It's a sin. You're not gay.

A girl walks in front of me; I slap her ass. She turns, angrily, then smiles as I apologize and say I'm drunk. I'm lucky. She must not have had a boyfriend or he probably would have kicked my ass.

What the hell am I doing? The screen on my phone illuminates.

Hey Josh, not really. Just hanging out on the couch. You?

Frankie, you sure? I can be there in five minutes.

The clipped, nervous thrusts inside my rib cage echo in my eardrums, and the unexpected moisture on the back of my neck catches the warm breeze. Nick and Mel slowly fade into more 20-somethings, cross the street, and finally I cannot point them out any longer. The cell in my hand remains dark; I'll just walk that way and if he doesn't answer, then I'll go home. It's only a minute out of the way. Not even really out of the way depending on how you look at it.

I check my phone again.

Frankie, what the hell are you doing to me? I should have known better. There's no way he's interested in me. I stop and look at my reflection in the window of an empty storefront. It's nearly impossible, no it is impossible, trying to be objective about your own appearance. I wouldn't classify myself as fat, but I'm not skinny either. Frankie is hot. He works out. I could see the muscles move under his shirt.

I've looked worse than I have tonight, and some would say I'm handsome, average or something. Maybe rugged. My scruff is at a good place this evening.

I'm stupid. He was just being nice. Flirting. It can kill you from the inside, and you don't even realize that it's happening until you can't move away from the words. Sticks and stones, and all that crap. Words do hurt.

My hair looks like shit. I should have tried a little harder.

He invited you out for you, just calm down. He saw what you looked like tonight, not any other night when you tried harder.

Still no messages.

I try to push the front of my hair back but one strand won't stay. Damn it.

A square of light brightens in my pocket, and I grab for the phone, fumbling. Fantasies of the screen smashing on the sidewalk quickly appear. It's saved and much less dramatic than I make it out to be.

Damn.

I feel bad for being disappointed that it's Josh. He's so sweet to me, and cute.

I really liked hanging out with you last night. I'm sorry if I'm being forward, or too much. You just seem really cool. Do you think we can do it again?

Don't do it. It was a one-time thing that you can't let happen again.

Frankie is the last.

Go hang out.

You can't do this. Your family will never forgive you. God won't forgive you. My stomach is rumbling, an uncomfortable, twisting pain.

Just got to the bar, you here yet? Frankie finally texts.

My cheeks stretch to their maximum capacity, but I hesitate to respond. Go home. Just go back to your place and go to sleep. Nothing good can come from this. You need sleep.

Two minutes.

Damn it, just go home and go to bed.

I shove the darkened phone back into my pocket and continue walking towards *Revolver.*

Ezra. Go home.

The florescent gun towers only slightly above the Victorian homes that surround the club. I've been there with friends from work a few times, but this isn't the same as that. This is me choosing to go, on my own, to meet someone. It's technically a gay bar but everyone goes. It's trendy, somewhat hipster, and you could make the case for it being simply "popular."

It's going to be fine. No one is going to question why you are here. There are a ton of gay people in town, and you worked with a bunch for years. No one will wonder; if they do, who cares. It's not a big deal.

-It's not a big deal, I whisper.

I hesitate when I see the crowd smoking out front, circling a raised, brick fire pit. The smoke from the small cigarettes climb and intermingle with the greater plume from the fire in the center. My breathing deepens again as I pull up my phone to ask Frankie's location. My assumption already is that it will take him a bit to answer, and I'm right, so I begin walking, looking at my phone to prove that I am indeed searching for someone and not hanging out at the bar alone.

The patio is brick, unaligned, old but new; my shoe snags a couple of times on jagged edges and I keep my head down. Quick glances have yet to reveal Frankie near the bar. Another glance at my phone. You would think it was a treasure map at this point with the multitude of times my eyes have met the screen.

-Wasn't sure I would actually get you to come out, Frankie says laughing. You seemed shy? Maybe mysterious.

His smile is mischievous.

I try to avert my gaze from his dimples, from the stubble that barely covers them, and from the way that he's looking at me. He kisses me on the cheek, softly, and pushes by me to get to the bar.

-What do you want?

This same question has been posed to me several times this evening, and it draws an unanticipated reaction: more stomach rumbling, cold sweats. Unusual, but not bad.

-Uh, I dunno. Bud Light.

He turns to face a bartender and I can no longer hear what he is saying but the muscles in his back meet the ones at the base of his neck in a jovial manner. I focus on the side of the bartender's head that is shaved, then change focus to the opposite side, platinum locks reaching her tattooed shoulder. I'm not sure how I would feel about this on another woman, but she pulls it off. A dark maroon vine grows from underneath her hair and encircles her spine. She reaches for several bottles at once, then a cocktail shaker, and sets it all down in front of Frankie.

-What are you doing, dude, I ask.

-Dude? He laughs and continues: I am getting you wasted.

-And why are you doing that?

-I'm a bartender, it's what I do, he says, that mischievous grin on display once again.

-Not here you're not, I counteract.

I hope I'm coming off as snarky and funny, not a douche. I can never tell, especially when I've had a good amount of alcohol. How much have I had tonight? Frankie pivots, grins, and hands me two shots over the head of a couple of guys.

-What are these, I ask.

-Just take them! They'll help you *really come out* tonight! He grabs my ass cheek as he says this and I pull away quickly, nearly spilling the blue shot before I can get it to my mouth.

Take the shot and get out of this situation before it gets worse. And, go! It's sweet, but not too sweet. I can't identify exactly what it is.

-What do you think?

-It's good.

-Awesome, have another, he yells pulling a second shot from behind his back.

-Dude! What are you doing to me?

-We'll get to that later, he winks.

Should I go home?

Of course, you should go home, you never should have come here.

I can't stop smiling.

Go home, go home, go home! You've told yourself that over and over and you haven't done it yet. Just admit that you are having a good time. What about Josh? Why am I ignoring him? Frankie hands me my beer and another small glass.

-You're not going to know what hit you tomorrow, sir, he says.

-I'm sure it's going to feel like a train. I take the shot and feel a hand on my shoulder.

-Hey! How's your night, Josh asks.

Shit! I forgot he was here. I'm so stupid.

Say something. I can feel a smile only appear for a moment before retiring fully into embarrassment.

-It was kind of last minute, I finally say. I was out with a group of friends for dinner and decided to stop in for a drink. You said you'd be here, and I thought I'd surprise you.

When did I become this kind of guy? The liar. Spare his feelings. Am I really, though, or am I pushing my guilt.

He looks at the row of empty glasses on the wooden bar.

-Or six, I continue.

He laughs, reaches to hug me, and says: Well, it's good to see you again.

I can feel myself pull back slightly and I hope he doesn't notice. Frankie turns, smiles, and reaches his hand to introduce himself.

-I'm Josh. It's good to meet you, he returns the greeting.

-You too. Have you known each other long?

-Actually, we just met last night, I interject.

-You're meeting a lot of friends these days, aren't you, Frankie remarks, sarcastically, jabbing my arm with his elbow.

I stand there letting the music overtake any possible silence and watch the uncomfortable look on Josh's face. Frankie shifts his focus back to the bar and puts a finger in the air.

-Are you having fun, Josh asks.

-So far; I just got here a few minutes ago actually. Are you meeting up with people?

-Nah, I just decided that I needed to get out of the house.

-Work tomorrow?

-Actually, I work for myself. I'm an architect.

-I guess I didn't think to ask that last night, did I?

-Actually, you did—twice, he said laughing.

-Wow, I can't believe you want to still talk to me. I'm such a mess!

-Yeah, but you're a cute mess.

My cheeks rise, stretching my mouth.

Josh's eyes are bright, captivating. Looking away would be the normal thing to do, but it feels wrong. I remember now why I was so happy when he texted me today.

Frankie turns and I smile. They are both attractive, far out of my league. They should be going for one another.

What is wrong with me? There is no way that they could be interested in me. They just want sex. That's it. They can tell that I like the attention, that if they get me drunk enough, I won't have the sense to say no.

Don't think about it. I pull out my phone and look at the screen.

Mom: I hope you have a good week. Love you.

He's gonna be gay. Is that what you want?

I move my head back and forth, trying to sync up with the music for consistency, but really trying to force the voice out. His voice. The music seems loud, too loud; but, it's not loud enough. Someone bumps into me and beer spills on my hand. An irrational heat rises into my face, my chest, and I glare at the culprit. Only the back of a brunette head is visible.

Why do girls even come to a place like this? Frankie's lips are moving and I have no idea if he has been talking to me or Josh. He should be talking to Josh; they're a match, far better than I with either one.

-What, I say loudly, embarrassingly loud.

Two sets of eyes, and two awkward smiles focus on me. Josh begins to laugh. Welcome to the conversation, he says.

-Sorry, I got distracted.

-By that girl behind you, Frankie asks. Didn't think you would be into that!

Frankie slaps me on the shoulder and laughs loudly.

-She spilled my damn drink.

-Whoa, killer!

I guess the girl heard me because both Frankie and Josh looked over my shoulder and chuckle.

Sorry, she says in a snarky tone. I hear her mutter "stupid fag" under her breath; the laugher quickly stops.

-What the fuck did you just say, Frankie yells, standing abruptly from his stool by the bar.

-Nothing, the girl says without facing us, a smile drawn across her face in the mirror.

-We all heard you, Josh interjects.

The girl finally turns, hitting me in the face with her hair. She screams: leave me the fuck alone!

Frankie steps forward and I move in front of him, looking to the bartender for help. He rushes over and I order a round of shots for the three of us. The bottle of brown liquid shakes in his hand slightly, each small glass losing a little. I grab them and practically throw one to Josh and Frankie.

-Let's do this, guys! Woo!

I skip taking a breath and let the burn quickly overtake my throat. The glass clicks on the stone bar before I decide to look up. I can't explain it other than it must have been the liquor because the girl was no more. She had taken her hatred somewhere else and the guys were laughing. Two empty glasses met in a line next to my own.

-Thanks, that hit the spot, Josh nearly screamed.

-Hey Ez, what are you doing here?

I can't place the voice, but I know it. A revenant bringing me back to reality.

I should not be in this place. This is not right. It's against the authority of God. At least that's what has been drilled into my head. I thought I'd escaped the prisons and trappings of a small town, only to enter another, smaller one that is my heart, my mind. You carry it with you, whether you want to or not.

When I was young, I dunno how old, maybe 12 or 13, some age where I thought I had apt opinions on topics I knew little to nothing about, there was some debate about homosexuals in the church. It might have simply been about them pastoring a church, but it was a mess. People threatened to leave. In fact, I believe some walked out that Sunday.

It's not something that I understood at the time, but the hatred, that I could feel.

That can't be right, though. That's not something we learned. Don't judge others; that's the right lesson. But the images of fire, and trying to contemplate the true length of eternity, that's pure fear.

So what, do you choose love, or something else? Even now, as an adult, I don't know what to do. Letting down God is too much to bear, though we do it every single day. We can't live up to perfection, and He knows that, and forgives.

-Ezra?

I turn slowly, my hands are moist, hot, fingers slipping off my palm.

-Hey Jamie, I muster after a moment to remember his name.

-What are you doing here? It's good to see you! How are you?

There's no accusation in his tone, simply a hello. But I know him better than this, I'm sure it's there.

He reaches in with both arms as I offer a hand. It's awkward, and his eyes show it. I offer the second arm in a semi bro hug. It still feels off and we retract quickly.

-I'm good. I'm actually just hanging out with a couple of buddies of mine.

I turn and gesture to Frankie and Josh at the end of the bar.

-How are you doing, I question.

-I've been good.

He smiles and watches me intently before asking the age old, "how long has it been?"

-I dunno. I mean I quit the restaurant six, seven years ago, so it's probably been about as long. Right?

I stutter over the time it's been. I'm not actually sure of the specifics. That's a lie, I am, but I don't want to seem like I care about that period in my life. It's behind me now, the reckless youth.

-What are you up to these days, I continue.

-I'm working as an Executive Assistant for a law firm, right now. What about you?

-That sounds interesting. Do you like it? I'm actually doing some office work myself, managing the day to day operations.

The fakeness in my own voice is not something I remember hearing in recent years. This was the atmosphere at the restaurant. Immature, and mean. I don't know how any of us did it. I don't even know the reason we treated each other the way we did.

It was a clique, and the need to belong proved strong, acutely so.

-Isn't that crazy? I can't believe it's been six years. It's easy to think of us as old now, I guess, he says laughing.

-And believe me, I feel like it a lot of the time, I half-heartedly interpolate.

My heart beats faster, and I long for this to be over. As much as I try to fight, this puts me back there.

-Me too!

-Are you dating one of those guys?

-What? No.

I turn and look quickly, then face Jamie again. I'm looking down at his forehead, the gray spot in his black hair, anywhere but his eyes.

-They are just buddies of mine, I continue.

The dampness flows from the pores on my forehead and I try to figure out which is greater, the need to wipe it away, or the need to look calm. Jamie and I were friends once, or at least acquaintances that would hang out on occasion. Innumerable bad habits had derived from this 'friendship', ones that I do not care to have brought up now. I became an asshole, and it's an image I have not been completely able to shed to this day. I found the humor in degrading others, but it made me part of the group. Part of some deranged family.

-I was actually headed to the bathroom, do you care if I stop on the way back through, I ask.

-Not at all. What are you drinking?

I look down at the blue and white label.

-Bud light it is, he says and turns towards the bar.

Once out of eyesight, I pull the back of my hand across my forehead and wipe the excess sweat on my jeans. The room has become stiflingly hot, and I realize the temperature has risen even more outside. The front doors are open, and the warm air saunters in, combining with the fiery heat inside. The smell of this many bodies intermingling begins to take precedence over anything else, even the various colognes.

I find my place in line behind three other men, waiting in solidarity for one purpose. Maybe one of two, I think. I laugh at myself and catch the meathead in front of me staring before quickly turning my head to face the bar and dance floor, to face Jamie, now talking to the bartender.

Don't go back to that now. You've cut those ties. The crazy way they thought they showed love and friendship was more possession than anything. You were one of them until you crossed them, or even said something that they didn't like. Rarely, you were even sure what crime you had committed.

I committed a crime of some sort in their eyes, and I was punished severely, exiled in the eyes of people that were once called friend. I had seen it before; they had done it to others, yet I was still surprised that the noose had been placed on my own neck.

-Get the A/C turned on, a burly gentleman says to one much younger and smaller as they push past the line of bathroom-goers.

It seems each year, or every other year, we get a version of this Indian summer. This one came from nowhere, though, completely unexpected, yet welcome. The snow from the previous week now lingered only in small piles at the edge of parking lots and sidewalks. So many things change in just a moment.

My gaze once again finds Jamie as he shoots two back-to-back shots, followed by a sip of beer. Another beer waits next to him, for me, I suppose.

I can't get sucked back into that world. I don't want to be that person anymore. The old cliché, or adage, or whatever it is that it's easier said than done is true. I've never been the same since I let myself get caught up in that world, and I know it was all me. My conscience seems to have broken, or at least timed out. I spend a lot of mornings telling myself that I am going to be different that day only to find myself falling back into old habits, judging people based on appearance.

I pray to God He can find grace and forgive me for all the wrongs that I have done. There have been so many.

Perhaps today is the worst that it's ever been? My willingness to fight has reached its lowest and I long to find happiness. I'm so very tired of fighting against the world, whether it be my perception or in truth. I just want a moment of joy, of something that doesn't include anxiety and guilt. My body, my mind are both worn down.

Josh and Frankie are out of sight now, but I picture Josh's smile. And Frankie's arms. How can something that feels this natural be against nature? I have struggled so hard against this. Ever since those first curiosities as a child developing into man, thinking about the other guys in high school and telling myself it's unforgiveable. I love God, more than anything, and letting Him down is not what I would ever want. Is loving a man wrong?

And I hope, no pray, that I still have a heart. I hope that I can find it again beyond all the bull in which I find myself buried.

-I think you are good to go, a thick, deep voice nudges me forward from behind.

I stammer off a thanks and push the bathroom door open, finding my way to the only free urinal in the corner.

Why do I feel that everything I do is wrong? Is it? Or does it just seem like that because others see things differently than I do. The position that I now find myself in, is in a word: fallen. I've fallen from the morals that I had prided myself on, but isn't pride another sin? Things used to be so simple, but were they? Ignorance is bliss.

Wash my hands, soap, water, dry, almost too quickly, but there's someone behind me waiting to do the same. One deep breath, then another, then open the door. I should have waited until I was in the small hallway, as the smell of shit overtakes me and I gag. The hall seems much shorter than I remember, hastening the time it is going to take me to get back to Jamie.

Don't fall back into that trap. You are stronger than the credit you are given. You've kept your mouth shut for years, and now is not the time to open it again. They'll try and take everything away again. They'll try and take your soul.

Just smile. Being friendly isn't wrong. Just smile, and you won't have to see him again if you choose.

-Hey, sorry that took so long, there was a line.

-That's what happens in a gay bar, he says laughing. The men's line is excessive and the girl's line is virtually nonexistent. Here's your drink.

I take the beer from him and take a long gulp. It feels cool and refreshing against my throat; what did I drink last? The time is accelerating and I can't keep track of how long I've been here.

-Where are your friends at, I ask.

-On the patio.

-I don't think I even saw there was a patio here.

-Yeah, it's out back, there.

He points to a door in the far left corner that I hadn't even noticed before, not even when I made my way past to the restroom only moments before.

-I know lots of smokers, he said casually, yet unnecessarily.

I don’t care.

-Thanks for the drink, but I had better get back to my buddies. They thought I was just going to the bathroom.

-They’re both really cute. Be careful, Jamie says and winks.

It was supposed to be a joke, but it didn’t seem that way. My phone buzzes in my pocket before I can make it back to the guys at the end of the bar. Jamie has friend requested me on Facebook. I thought I had blocked him, but it has been so many years, it’s hard to say for sure.

-Where the hell have you been, Frankie yells and slurs when he sees me five feet away.

-I ran into someone I used to know. How much have you had, sir, I ask.

-Not enough! Now get us some shots! You need to get on this level.

-Okay, then!

9:15PM

My head is only slightly pounding as the darkness opens and surrounds me. What the hell happened? This is not a room, or my own apartment. I do not recognize the sound of a radiator or wind from a ceiling fan. Adjusting my eyesight to the darkness is harder than I would imagine that it should be, but I am hungover, or drunk, I don't even know at this point. The red, block numbers at the side of the bed let me know that it is now 9:18.

Is that AM or PM? I would assume PM but can't be sure.

The heat to each side of my body is not a concern until I move my arms in each direction and find another human, breathing deeply, satisfied with their own evening and sleep.

What did I do?

My head falls onto the warmth of a pillow, my neck unable to muster the strength to hold it up any longer. Did I shake the bed? Don't wake anyone up. Figure out what is going on first, who you are with.

I hear snoring, but I can't tell which body it is coming from, maybe both. My eyes have not adjusted to the darkness enough to recognize facial features. My eyelid catches on my contact. After two fingers hold my eyes open long enough for the lenses to fall back in place, I rub back and forth with my fist and will my eyes to see better, faster. Frankie is to my left; I turn my head, only my head, and see Josh.

What am I doing?

What the hell is happening with me?

I've got to get out of here. How the fuck do I do that without waking them? Maybe it's not a problem, they're cool guys.

I stop for a moment and look at Josh's face. He's smiling, or something close to one is drawn ever so slightly on his lips. That smile that I saw this morning, the one that made me feel different. The one that made me feel like maybe it's okay to give in and let these feelings happen. My fingers find a spot on his cheek and pull downwards from the cheek to the dimple in his chin. I close my eyes and let my lips meet his. I'd already forgotten how soft they were and how good it felt.

For a moment, I just want to reach out and pull his arms around me. I want him to tell me that everything is going to be fine, this isn't a sin. It's okay to want to be cared for, to feel something for once that isn't guilt or worry. There are hours left of darkness, but it doesn't feel like it could ever be enough. We could hide here in the black. We could find love in the emptiness, because that's what this is?

Right? It's dark, it's unnatural.

Stop doing this to yourself.

Josh stirs and his tongue wipes my kiss from the top lip, then the bottom. I'm sure it unfolds slower in my mind than in reality. I want to see his eyes, the ones that saw me for who I am. The ones that saw my deepest secret and somehow brought it out of me, the ones that saw into my soul.

Did I really just think that? Am I drunk still? I'm not a teenage girl that's for sure. Stifling a cough is harder than it should be. There's no need to face them yet. It's too soon. I need to get out of here without them knowing.

The morning is coming. It always does, and I am going to be faced with the fact that I don't even know who I am anymore. I've got to get out of here. I slowly sit up in the bed and let my eyes move to each side of the room, getting to know what details my intoxicated mind can take in.

The only thing covering my body is a pair of boxers. Where are my clothes? There are several small piles lying to the foot of the bed, any one of those could be mine. It's unlikely the temperature has dropped too much considering it will climb even higher today. It was almost sixty the last time that I checked my phone.

When was that, though? It could have been hours.

The bed shakes slightly as I slide my legs and ass to the bottom of the bed like a worm. My toe confirms that the floor is carpeted, which is good for me. That will make less noise as I try to free myself into the night. Just do this in parts, Ezra. It's going to be fine.

Part one: get out of the bed. It's done.

Part two, find my phone to use the light. I start with the bedside table next to Josh, letting my hand only subtly touch each object. Nothing. I make way to the other side of the bed. Frankie's side. I can see his muscular chest rising and falling. He's the one snoring. I find two phones on this table and pray that one of them is mine.

The center button on the first phone brings to life my background. I pick it up and use it above the various piles of clothes that are all over the floor. Dammit! They're mixed together. Why can't something be easy?

Not sure I deserve anything to be easy after what I've done.

I start pulling them apart, quickly, and as quietly as possible. I find my shirt first, then my jeans, and then my coat. I reach for the back pocket and feel the leather square. The keys are still in the side pocket. It looks like I've managed to keep ahold of everything I'd left my house with earlier in the day. The belt buckle echoes only slightly and I grab it quickly. I pull the door to the room open two minutes later and look at the two sleeping men before pulling it slowly closed.

The hall light leads me down a tight staircase to the main floor; the house is old, very old. I zip my coat, turn the lock on the doorknob, and pull it closed behind me. I don't want to be responsible if some stranger walks in the front door and takes everything.

It's quiet but warm as I walk down three stairs to the sidewalk, tripping slightly on a protruding root. Why do I always do that? I'm exhausted but strangely refreshed. The house looks dark from the sidewalk across the street, and I wonder when they will realize that I am gone.

The buildings around me look familiar and I can see the towering structures of downtown against the sky to my right. I live to the left of them as well so I'm on the right side of town. The battery symbol shows red in the corner of my screen and I quickly pull up the maps, entering my address while trying to watch my surroundings.

Just a few blocks away, and things should be more recognizable at the next major road. I put my phone away and follow the direction it had just given me. There are many strange noises, but questionably, no fear.

What do I have to fear? Anything bad would be punishment, right?

For a moment my vision is blurred, but the water soon falls down my cheek. I wipe it away and keep walking. There is no reason for me to be upset. I've got a good life. I made a couple of mistakes, but I can move away from them. Why do I keep thinking that? The tears begin to fall a little harder and I do my best to keep them quiet. I am not sure exactly who I am trying to hide them from. There is no one else on the street.

Each block of concrete is only slightly larger than my normal stride, and I extend it accordingly to make sure my feet only touch the lines. The tears soon dry from my face, and the warm night breeze caresses my cheek. I pull up the sleeves of my coat and roll up the bottoms of my jeans.

Take advantage of the warmth while you can. There's no way it will last too long. I should pay attention to the weather more, I mean, there's an app on my phone. Did they predict this? I feel like I went over this earlier in the night, but everything is hazy. I close the app containing directions since I now know where I am and look at the screen. The text message box says I have no messages.

An extreme sort of disappointment hits me harder than I thought it might; the tears come again, and a little harder.

Fucking stop. Don't be a little bitch about this, man.

My place. It's just behind the white, vine-covered house that will most likely be rubble by the end of summer. Something deeper than anticipation builds inside, almost a longing just to be inside four familiar walls. There has been too many unknown places today. I let them take the safety net from beneath and I'm wobbling on the wire, looking down, wondering just when I'm going to fall. I grip the doorknob tightly while fiddling for my keys. It seems weird, even to myself, but what's the point of more questions?

My sanity seems to have taken leave of me at some point today. I have learned to love myself a little less each day for a couple of decades now, but I feel like this is a new contempt, a new deprecation on the level of a psychopath. A self-destructive tendency that I worry will never end.

Looking back, it seems that I have been on this path for some time. The blackouts. Lost periods of time that all started as fun.

Fun.

I'm not sure that I'm even having that any longer. My body feels older when I partake in these collegiate activities; it is older, but not necessarily wiser as predicted. Any recovery that takes less than a full day has become a near miracle. It takes several to feel normal in most cases. I hate it, but I let myself do it over and over again.

When did I become just another drunk? Is that even what it should be called in this case? It's more of a binge. A bender to forget the pain that continues to build upon itself day after day. A binge to block out feelings that I have been told should not be inside of my heart in the first place.

I often wonder how long someone can live with this anxiety before the heart can't take it anymore. There are days that I sit back in my chair at work and think maybe this will be the day that it gives out.

The screen is about to go black, and as it does, it hits me that I still have to work tomorrow. I don't care. I just don't care, anymore.

A chill digs into my body and up my back, my body shivering. No source reveals itself upon facing the street. No wind. I drop my keys on the hall table and fall down onto the heating vent. The air warms me and I fall onto my side. I'm so tired. Too tired. The idea of leaving this spot for anything feels impossible.

I need to sleep. That's it; just sleep for days. Locked up inside these walls. I am safe here.

There's no temptation inside my home, my sanctuary. The cold floor feels good against my cheek. I remember this from childhood, sitting near the heat, wrapped in a blanket. It was a radiator then. The hum lulled me to sleep on cold nights.

I miss my mom. It's been too long since I have been home, and I wish she was here to hug me, to hold me. I'm far too old for that, but I think it's something that we all need from time to time. This is probably the final time I'll be able to check the digital numbers on my cell. It's too late to call, anyway.

She'll answer.

I hear the level-headed voice somewhere inside and reply that it's not right to do that to her. She has to be awake in the morning for work, and the last thing that she needs is another drunk call in the middle of the night. She's dealt with that for too many years with my father, and I can't end up like that. No matter what I can't be that burden on her.

He left her; he left us in the only way that it seems he could have. He left before any of his business was done. He went into the ground with so many unanswered questions, both mine and maybe his own. He knew so little about me. Didn't care to know more, I assume.

I know that he loved me in his own way.

I hope that he loved me, even if it was in his own way.

She won't walk away from you like he did. Mothers are different. They care.

I don't want her to have to make that choice. If anything, I will make the choice for her. She shouldn't have to live with the thought that her son has become just another in a long line predicated at birth to become drunkards just because that's how it's always been.

She loved him at one time, but is love unconditional when you choose to give it? Is all love just conditional? Was there a time I knew how they met and got together? If so, it has escaped me now. I can't let her know about any of this, not the drinking, not this secret. These questions and doubts are my own. She's far too good a person to have to handle it, but I think she would.

Would she?

Yes, and that's the problem. She doesn't deserve any of it.

I won't hurt her. Not anymore. I had my issues before, but I conceal them now. There's no reason to worry her. She did everything that she could to save me from the mental scars that I have somehow let rise to the surface. She has let the past go. I try, but I'm stuck with it, mired in a pit of regrets and loneliness. I have somehow become a proud victim, but how do you make peace with a ghost?

Victim is the last word that I would ever want associated with me. I don't want people to feel sorry for me, so I will shove it all down. I will medicate myself into a false smile, a smile that people have grown to know as my real one. Hell, I'm not sure if I remember what the real thing looks like anymore.

It's easy to think something when that's what you want it to be. No one really cares that on the inside I am still losing it. One day the madness may truly get me, but until then, I will continue to walk down this narrow path that society has set in front of me because no one wants to hear my problems. The world has become too self-serving, myself included. It's really a conundrum that I can't figure out. If we spent more time listening to people and trying to help them, maybe they would do the same for others. The world would then become a little less self-serving.

Is that right? It's all sounds so simple—too simple.

The pounding in my head has deepened, penetrating the space behind my eye sockets. The task of getting myself from the floor is more difficult than the actual walk to the kitchen. I look at two identical wooden cabinets deciding which one to open. I know which one is the smart choice but tonight that's not what I want. Tonight, I am going to take this road, the dangerous, broken road, and see where I end up. If it kills me, then that's what's going to happen.

I have no idea where I heard it, but maybe it would be better to become a fond memory than a current worry. I'm not even sure if that's how I heard it. I open the cabinet to the immediate right of my refrigerator and pull out the bourbon, its slick glass reflecting the light from the hallway. My body cannot handle the full immersion of the kitchen lighting.

The glass echoes throughout the lower level when I accidentally hit it against the container. It falls to the floor, shattering, dying.

Don't break the bottle, idiot!

I laugh out loud and worry about waking someone. Who am I going to wake? I'm alone. I'm always alone here.

The cabinet is close to get another, but I pull my hand back midway. I twist the cap off the clear bottle and throw back my head, the spout touching my lips. A bubble of liquid hesitates momentarily in the back of my throat before slipping into my stomach. I place the bottle back on the counter and stand still. Perfect stillness will increase the chances that vomit will not make its way into my throat and onto my floor.

There have been innumerable nights of practice for this. More guilt should begin in my stomach before rising to my chest over this fact, but what do I have left to lose tonight? The feeling goes away and I grab the bottle once again, letting myself slide down the wall onto another heating vent. The warm air feels good, but I can feel the sweat start to form on my forehead. It's too warm for the heat to be on, but it feels right.

The sweat begins to form again in other parts of my body. Turning down the heat seems impossible from the position I currently find myself sitting in on the floor. After a few minutes, I realize I am still wearing my coat, so I remove it and lay it on the floor.

That will make a great pillow later, I laugh.

Another drink, this time longer than the first. I feel my body begin to convulse with laughter. What the fuck am I doing? I look at my phone. It's later and the battery even lower, the symbol glaring red. The connection has turned itself off in order to preserve the little energy that is left in the small device.

-I don't think I am going to make it to work tomorrow. Today? I don't know. Ha!

More liquor and the wetness runs down my chin, dripping from what I like to call a beard onto my shirt at the collarbone. Dammit. I sit the bottle down and push myself forward, stumbling in an attempt to stand. Somehow, this set of intoxicated acrobatics is managed with no harm to my body.

I look at the stairs to the back of the kitchen pondering for a moment on distance. The bathroom in the front hallway is closer. My shoulder bounces off the wall several times, each incident with varying degrees of pain.

Where is the switch? I have turned this on thousands of times, but you would think I had never been here before. Stranger in my house.

The reflection I am afforded once illumination is present is not the one that I remember from the beginning of the night. My hair has taken on the look of a desert tumbleweed.

I like it, though. It seems to lay better, look better when it's not totally of my doing.

My cheeks have turned scarlet, which I am not sure which to attribute this to, the wind, the heat, or the whiskey.

Probably all three.

There is a dark spot on my neck that I turn my head to examine. It's difficult to see at this angle. The teenager in me immediately recognizes the bruise-like mark. I cannot contain the laughter that now fills the bathroom.

-Who am I, right now?

How many times have I had to ask myself that question in the last couple of days? Even I'm bored with it.

He's going to be a fag! Is that what you want?

I close my eyes and cover my ears. My father's voice.

-Shut up! You don't get to say that! You never even got to know me!

My hand leaves a print on the mirror as I pull it back. I look at my face again. This is not what I want. This is not something I chose. Why would I choose this? It's going against everything that I have ever been taught to believe. Everyone is going to hate me; they're going to be disgusted by me. I just want to talk to my mom. I just need to talk to her.

I stumble from the bathroom and to the floor where I left my phone. I look at the screen. It's too late to call her and the connection is closed.

Where is my fucking charger?

Just leave her alone. I can feel the tears again. My vision is blurred and I grab the bottle from the floor. Another swig. Another. Another. She doesn't have to know about this. Just let her love you like she thinks you are now, happy and healthy. You won't survive if she hates you. You can't survive if she hates you. Another drink. Another.

I begin to walk in circles, my head fuzzy.

Keep a clear mind.

No, don't keep a clear mind. Drink more. Just make everything stop. I need to talk to someone. I can't do this on my own.

Who's going to answer the phone? I am alone. I pull my phone to my face and open my contacts list.

Mel: *Are you awake?*

Nick: *Hey.*

John: *You awake?*

Kayla: *What's going on?*

Lindsay: *Hey.*

The texts sit there. No connection.

-Fuck!

Where is my charger? I find it curled in the corner and plug the phone in quickly. The messages sit there, and I throw the phone onto the counter before reaching for the bottle.

How long have I been walking around my house. The bottle is gone and it feels like hours. Maybe minutes only. What time was it when I plugged in my phone?

I don't even remember who all I have texted, but they seem to have gone through. My phone is now at 30% battery life.

I have to get out of here. I'm hot. I can't breathe. I hold my hand to my face; it's shaking. Please stop. How do I make it stop? Just open the door and go. You can't be here, Ez! You need air.

The bourbon bottle is empty as I let it drop into the trashcan. I already knew it was empty, right? Who cares?

I grab my keys and lock the front door. My garage is across the street from my townhouse. The door rises from silence when I enter the code into the keypad. It's still warm. I pull my buttoned shirt off and sit there for a moment in my t-shirt.

-This isn't a good idea, Ez. This is a fucking stupid idea!

I don't care; I have to get out of here. The radio comes to life playing a song that I don't think I know. It must be new. I change the station until I find something that I do know. An oldie. I can't remember who sings it. I turn my head and wipe my eyes, trying to see behind me. I let my foot off the brake and my sedan begins to move in reverse. There are no issues with this. I slam the stick into park and watch the door fall into place.

-Maybe there's no turning back, and maybe I'm wrong, I sing loudly.

I don't even think that those are the correct lyrics, but it's how I am feeling.

It's hard to describe, really, even to myself. Maybe, it's the state I'm in, or maybe it's just that complicated for me. Or, I'm stupid.

I feel hopeless. I have literally become something that is hated by many. I'm not sure I have it in me to live like that. I've tried to pretend I don't care what people think of me, but I do. Can anyone really live with that much hate pointed towards them? I'm weak. I want to be strong more than anything; I always have. I spent my entire childhood being strong, smiling on the outside while I languished in the destruction inside. I turn at the stop sign and push the gas to accelerate onto the freeway.

Let it go. This is your chance. You've been thinking about it all day; just turn around and let it go. There's no need to kill yourself to prove something.

-Maybe, I do.

Maybe, that's all I have left, the only way to take back my life is to end it.

I'm so tired of the depression, and the loneliness. Others telling me how I should be feeling and who I should be in love with. So tired of having no idea what I really want out of life. My mind is constantly working, constantly anxious. I'm taking several small breaths and my chest feels like it is going to explode. Just stop. This is your chance to stop all of this. I look down and I'm going eighty; I pull back on my foot to slow down some. If I get arrested, I'm fucked either way. Worse so than before.

Still no messages pop up on my phone.

It's only midnight; they aren't asleep. Maybe this is the sign that I need. Real friends are not something that I have been able to find. I somehow have ended up in this cycle of repetition. They tell you in high school that this isn't what life is going to be like, but that's all life really is. It's a succession of high school, over and over. It's the nightmare you have as a teenager but assume one day you will actually escape. I know that's what I believed, but it's not getting better. Someone or something always comes before me when it comes to the people in my life. Even after I chose my friends more carefully, I managed to mess that up and almost completely lose the good person that I used to be.

And really, I don't even know how good that was. I've always had this innate selfishness. I'm not sure where that was learned other than my theory that I had to fight for any kind of attention I wanted. I somehow became one of those people that needed the approval of others to feel good about themselves. I would throw away perfectly good people from my life, all while chasing those who didn't give two fucks about me. It's been more apparent the last few years, and you'd think I was fifteen years old all over again.

This can be my decision now. I have made nothing but a mess of my life. Maybe. Just maybe.

Can I base a decision like this on all of these maybes? There are so many, but too many? I'm tired. I'm just so tired.

-Tired, I say out loud but cannot hear myself over the radio.

My eyes begin to glaze over and I blink them quickly. I check all three mirrors to make sure I have not alerted a cop or let my car slide into the opposite lane. There are no other headlights that I can see. None ahead or behind. The continuous yawns are making it hard to pay attention. Just stay awake. You're too far into this drive to turn around. I roll down the windows and turn up the music. I flip through the stations and finally hit SEEK. A techno beat makes me jump slightly. This should keep me awake for the rest of the drive.

-What are you doing?

Just leave her alone. She's sleeping and has to be up in the morning. You're only going to worry her. What are you even going to say? You drive home in the middle of the night, clearly drunk. She is going to freak! I can't do this to her.

I need to talk to her. I don't know what I'm going to say, but I need to just talk to my mom. She is going to make this okay. She always makes it okay.

She'll hate you.

-No!

She will.

-No, I yell louder.

She isn't going to hate me. She loves me no matter what!

He's going to be gay! Is that what you want?

Your. Son.

I don't even remember how old I was; probably mid-teens. I had looked at gay porn on the internet. I don't know why.

I do know why. I was curious. My dad had found the history, and I didn't know what to say. They fought about it after they thought that I had gone to bed. I could hear the yelling from my room upstairs, so I walked into the hallway and dropped down to the floor against the wall.

-It's disgusting, he had yelled. Is this what you want your son to be? It's wrong.

-He's just a kid, my mom had defended.

-You can't defend this! You saw what he was looking at!

-It's curiosity. Kids are curious.

-Bullshit! You know exactly what is going to come of this, same as I do!

I heard a door slam. There were footsteps on the porch and I heard a can hit the floorboards, roll, then stop against something indiscernible. A moment later the car started and the engine's sound faded quickly. Then I heard something that I didn't want to ever hear. My mom was crying. I could hear her saying, "please God," between the tears. From that moment on, I hid any curiosity that I had in me. I buried any feelings that I might have had. I wouldn't hurt her like that again. That was a promise I tried to keep. I fought with everything that I had.

I can't blame a dead man for losing my grip.

I think I've tried for years, even subtly. All I ended up doing was hurting me—and them.

The phone sits in my console between the two front seats. There has been no indication of life but I push down the center button anyway. Nothing; no one cares to answer. I've been here one too many times I assume. I've let the world get the best of me, and I don't want that anymore.

I just want to be happy, but how do you do that for yourself? I assume that at some point in my life I had some happiness. I was a happy child, I think. You don't live in complete, constant darkness. I must have blocked most of it out because right now all I can think of is the sadness, the rage. The alcohol.

How is it that a person can fully avoid happiness? I don't think that it's something I meant to do. It's probably not even possible, right?

I think that intermittently my self-destruction became a way of life, like a religion or custom that grips you so tightly that you begin to breathe it in and soon it's who you are. I pull my steering wheel to the left and exit the freeway, following the signs to a gas station that has seen better days. The lights of the neon sign flicker and stay off longer than they remain on. I would be nervous if I hadn't been here before. I pull a stick of gum from my glove box then grab another piece and shove it in.

My face looks normal to me in the rearview, but I'm drunk. I shouldn't be driving but sitting at home alone seems worse and more dangerous to myself than action.

The warm breeze flits across the top of some bushes at the corner of the small, wooden structure. They won't ask questions here. Just keep it together.

An old, haggard woman looks my way before returning her eyes to the magazine that's sprawled on a counter I'm sure has more germs than a toilet seat—or a cell phone, so I hear. I smile and walk towards the back, past the chips, and the random cardboard dinners that places like this stock for lonely bachelors. The inside of the freezers wheeze with age, and it's nearly impossible to see exactly what lies inside. The door handle is cold and I reach quickly for the 12 pack just inside. I rethink my decision and grab a box filled with 24 cans of beer.

I'm drunk, and I only plan to get drunker.

I don't care much anymore.

You've already made that clear, Ez. You don't care.

I need a break from thinking. My head is starting to hurt. The glass door slams closed and I rub deep into the area where my neck meets my skull. The woman pushes her scraggly hair behind her ear and does not immediately look up. She is finishing her story, some tabloid, but I can't tell anymore about it. She finally looks up and mutters, this all?

-Yeah.

I reach for my wallet and realize that I'm not breathing. I don't want her to smell my breath, not that she seems to care anyway. I assume that she works the night shift for a reason. Maybe, she likes to be alone with her thoughts, or maybe she's just lazy and this is the least amount of work. I don't know. It's not my place to judge, although I realize that is exactly what I am doing with these assumptions.

She reaches for my card and runs it through a small machine that sits just beside the ancient cash register. I'm not exactly sure what year the cash register was invented, but it seems this one was from one of the first few generations.

-Thanks, I say when my card is returned.

-Sure, have a good one.

She doesn't mean it; how could she? She doesn't even know who I am. Would she remember me, my face, if I turned up on the television in the morning? I'm sure if something terrible happened, she would remember, but otherwise, I'm part of a paycheck, some random guy who messed up her night by coming in to buy something. The chances she would come forward are slight in the event of an accident; she would be liable, selling me this beer.

I suddenly regret not looking for an energy drink while inside, but I am not going back in there. I don't want to ruin her celebrity gossip again, and going back would look mildly suspicious at this point. You had some good luck, Ez. Don't push it!

The case of beer fits nicely against the back of the passenger seat and I check my phone once again before even walking back to my side of the vehicle. No texts. I turn it off and throw it in the backseat. No one is going to care tonight unless they think I'm in trouble, and still, I'm not sure if I would get an answer then. The flap on the box of beer gives me some trouble, but I finally pull out a cold, silver can. It falls into the cup holder easily and I leave the parking lot. I doubt that woman would care, but it's better not to take any unnecessary risks by actually drinking it while still in the parking lot.

My raucous, heavy laughter fills the car and I turn up the radio. This whole damn night has been nothing but one big unnecessary risk. I am so damn drunk, I can barely see, but I found it a good idea to go for a drive? I know where I'm at, and I don't want to admit it to myself, but I just want to go home. I want to go back to being a kid again, but how much better was that?

Deep down my father must have known what I was going to become. Do you become gay? No, that's not right.

I'm sure he feared it. I know that I do.

Dear God, please help me understand this. This is not something that I want. Is this something that I am supposed to fight against, because I don't think I'm that strong. I don't think that I have much fight left in me. We aren't supposed to understand everything, but this might be too much for me. How is this not something that you are born with when so many think it's an abomination? I want it to be gone. I want to be normal. That's all I want.

I just want to be normal.

The coldness of the beer relieves the scratching in my throat momentarily. Another gulp only brings more relief to this pain that has been plaguing me all day, ever since I threw up the first time this morning. The beer clinks softly as it falls back into its cradle. A comfort to me tonight more so than ever before.

Remnants of short, brown corn stalks line each side of the highway. Two glowing eyes catch my attention, and a deer runs in front of my car from the opposite side of the road. I slam on the brakes and the back end of the car slides back and forth across the yellow line. Two does follow the first moments later; I couldn't get a look at what it was, but I imagine it was a buck.

My dad would have loved this.

It takes a moment, then two, but I breathe again, deeply, and fully aware of each inhalation. They are labored and harsh. I can feel my pulse in my neck. The animals have disappeared again into the field on the opposite side of the road. I grab the steering wheel and let my foot off the brake. The car moves back into my own lane and I continue, slower. Sobriety, or at least the temporary sensation, kicks in and I decide again reaching for another beer.

It takes another few minutes to realize that I am breathing routinely again and my typical speed has resumed. I'm still not sure that I care if something happens tonight, but do I want it to be some stupid accident? It could be the beer talking, but what if? What if maybe I should just give up? I've had some fun this weekend, but would I really want this to be my last one?

I suddenly feel as if I've had an energy pill. I am sitting straighter in the seat and the glaze from my eyes has gone. I look at the clock in the middle of my dashboard…

…1:50AM, Monday

There's plenty of time to make that decision if it comes to it. I turn right onto an invisible driveway lined with pine trees. It's impossible to know it's there if you weren't looking for it. A colder, unforgiving darkness takes over the area surrounding my car. For most, this would signal the beginning of a horror movie. For me, this is the beginning of the road home.

The crescent in the sky no longer finds its way to me or to the rocks I hear hitting the bottom of my car. The sounds of crickets and cicadas will be deafening this summer, and the thought of summer provokes a slight sadness. I watch both sides of the small, gravel driveway for more deer. I turn my lights to low just before I enter a deep curve, the last one before the main, towering structure comes into view. The white farmhouse looks gray against the night and still retains a touch of the grace it once held a hundred years ago. It's only the night, though, that gives it this effect. The night romanticizes and makes beautiful what the day illuminates and destroys.

The evergreens move steadily in the increasing wind and let just enough moonlight through to refract off the windows. I pull the car to the right side of the front porch and turn it off. The engine should be quiet enough that it doesn't draw attention from inside the house. I pull a beer from the case in the passenger seat and take a long drink.

-You've never let me down, I smirk to myself in the rearview and kiss the can before chugging the rest of it down.

I pull the tab on another and open the car door. The ground seems to be moving, but I'm drunk, not stupid. The thud of the door is louder than expected and I watch my mother's window for a light or any signs of movement.

There are none.

I walk to the front porch and stop at each stair to listen for the familiar creak of the old wood. I find my usual spot in the middle of the wooden porch swing and push off with my left foot. The small links in the chain clank against one another as the swing moves back and forth against the current of the wind. I close my eyes and smile. This place on the porch had become a place of revival for me as a child. A place of safety to find myself when my parents would fight.

The disappointment of failing your parents hits even harder when you are an only child. Perhaps that letdown was why they stopped after me. There's no one for that love and pride to fall back on. The next best thing, for a parent who isn't proud of you, is to forget, push you aside from their memory, from their very presence.

I'm sure my father tried to find something about me that he was proud of, but academia was not something that he cared about. It's not to say that I was over the moon about education, but it was something that I was good at, something in which I excelled with no trouble. You would assume that that had put me in a good position to be something in this world. I believed all of that crap when I was a kid, too.

The myth that just because you are bullied in school means you will grow up to do something great is just that, a myth. I'm nothing more than middle management. There is absolutely no greatness in that. My employees come and go each day, thinking little of the man sitting in the office nearby.

I'm not even sure where this need to be something special comes from? I know immediately this is a lie. I am lying to myself now. I assume that I get it from the fact that I wasn't able to live up to some imagined standards I had for myself. It's not even from another person. I had wanted so much for myself. I wanted that "American Dream" of fame and fortune, but sometimes it just never comes. Sometimes, you are just left with yourself and some mediocre talent you blow out of proportion and believe is special.

The screen door slams in its frame and I open my eyes quickly. That split second of me falling asleep had been enough for the wind to find itself behind the door. The breeze has grown stronger and it feels like the temperature has climbed even higher than anyone would have anticipated, even taking this warm front into account. The door slams again and I realize that I have winced.

I can still see my mother running from the house and into the yard, crying and holding her face. She had wiped the tears away quickly when she saw me.

-Hey, honey, what are you doing, she asked me, smiling.

-What's wrong, I had asked, ignoring her question.

-Nothing, sweetie, I'm fine.

-Mom, you're crying.

-I was cutting up onions to make a salad. I'm fine. I just wanted to come out and make sure that you were okay. You having fun?

-I'm fine, Mom. Even then I didn't believe her, but I was a kid. What can you do?

-What are you playing?

-Just practicing.

-Are you excited for the show tonight?

-Yeah!

-Nervous at all?

-Nah. Is Dad coming?

-Is AJ coming with you?

-Mom, you know AJ isn't real!

-To you, he is.

She had said this with such sincerity. I suppose she hadn't wanted to lose her child to a world that would turn out to be much crueler than I could have imagined at that age. How do you keep up the lie to a child that they can have the life that they want to live? I'm thankful for the chance that I had to dream of something great, but part of me, however small, wishes that I had been told that life would ultimately crush me.

I wish to God that I had wanted to be an engineer or something that actually could sustain me. More than sustain me, I suppose. I may have slowly killed my dreams, but I could have at least enjoyed the time that I didn't spend working. Now, all I have are regrets and a soul that may or may not have died a long time ago.

Damn, that was dramatic.

-I'm too old for an imaginary friend, I yelled. The authority in my voice was to prove that I was mature, or at least I thought I was. The idea that maturity was even a word I knew is laughable to me now.

-I'm going to finish dinner. Make sure you are ready for the play. We'll leave right after.

-Is dad going?

I knew the answer. She had avoided it the first time, but even as a child, I needed to hear the words. It was like an affirmation that I didn't warrant any of his precious time. She looked at me for a while in a way I couldn't describe at the time. There's so much that I don't remember from my childhood, but I remember that look. She had stood there, her hair blowing across her eyes. She hadn't tried to push it away. Thinking on it now, she had been crying.

-Is dad coming tonight, I repeated. Why didn't I stop? Why did I have to keep pushing her on the point? I didn't know then how much it hurt her, but that look. I know it now. I've seen it in the mirror. It's pain.

He had no interest in spending time with a son that didn't care about hunting or fishing or some other sport that I could only see as boring. It seemed like a lot of sitting around, waiting to kill something. That's not who I am, or who I ever wanted to be. It's not that I disapprove of any of it, but I just didn't want to participate. Maybe, he wanted the opportunity to hang out and talk. I can't imagine what we would have talked about, though.

Was I the selfish one? The one who didn't reach out to him?

-No, honey, he has to do something, she lamented, reaching out to pull me in close with both arms.

I smiled. I didn't know what else to do. The only thing I could think to say was: AJ can have his seat.

I watched her smile and I could hear her sharp breaths as she teared up again. Even at that age, I wanted to protect her. I wanted to make sure that she was happy, and the more I understood, or at least thought I understood, was that she was not happy with my father. I'm sure I don't know the full the extant of what lead to the unhappiness, and to be honest, I'm not sure that I ever want to know. What I do know is that she has the chance to be happy now. I don't want to take that away from her by ending up as the exact same person.

I find myself beside that same tree now, looking back at the house. That day was one of many that I'm sure fights erupted over me. My mom wanted my father in my life. He had his own wants, his own needs, and his own demons. Who knew that the one thing we would have in common would be the thing that my mom hated the most: drinking? I somehow picked that up along the way without ever really meaning for it to happen. It was around the time I had let the darkness of people who I would now describe as borderline sociopaths in. Not all of them; some were like me, I'm sure, just wanting to belong to something other than themselves. It was a quick fall to depths that I could never have imagined.

I let myself descend into a sitting position between the two massive roots that extend out further into the yard and try to pinpoint that moment when I lost everything that I had liked about myself.

Looking back over it, I don't think there really was one moment to pinpoint. It was many moments, over a few years that I let my guard down. I subconsciously decided that having friends meant more than having morals.

Those people are gone now.

They fell off along the way when the good still shone through the bad, and I didn't want to destroy others. There's no way to justify my actions, but what is self-pity going to get me? I can't lie about my past, but can I really walk into the future with my head held high? Do I have the strength for that? I know that God forgives, but what about this aspect of my own personality that I have discovered lies inside? That's not something that goes away.

Josh.

Frankie.

They are good people.

No, they are nice guys. I don't really know them at all, not the real them I could discover over time.

Is this a test? Do I deny myself happiness so that I can save my soul? Will this damn my soul?

-God, please. Help me. Save me. Show me what I need to do! I have no idea what I'm supposed to do! I'm losing my mind, here, and I can't do this on my own. Please.

At this point, I can barely understand my own words. I'm trying to keep the tears silent; I don't want my mom to know that I'm here. The desperate throbbing has once again taken up residence just behind my eyes. I can't fall asleep here. Mom will freak out if she finds me in the yard tomorrow morning. It takes a few deep breaths, but I finally muster the strength and push myself to my feet. My body wobbles back and forth and for a moment the ground spins. This subsides when I close my eyes for a few moments and lean against the rough bark.

The spinning finally stops completely and I make my way across the yard towards my car. The dew begins to soak into the bottom of my jeans, taking on more weight than I care to hold onto. I can't stand wet jeans, or any sort of wet clothes at all, I suppose. It's irritating and chafes against my body. I instinctively rub the inside of my leg for some imaginary itch that has not begun to surface.

The trip to the car seems much further than I remember, the yard morphing into a space I have never traversed. My body staggers back and forth as I make my trip, which now seems more like a journey since I cannot put one foot in front of the other. My foot finds a hole and I pray I won't feel that in the morning.

There are very few leaves on the ground, raked to the edge of the property; I wonder who she is having do that? I haven't been home as much as I probably should have lately, leaving her to take care of the old house. She's certainly capable of keeping up the place. She had me fairly young, as people tended to do in the eighties. Sometimes, I wonder if maybe it would be a good idea for her to sell the place. Put all the memories behind her, both good and bad, and just move on.

It was just my dad, mom, and myself, and now that he is gone, and I'm gone, it's just her. She doesn't need all the room and she commutes almost an hour to work. A nice apartment, or condo—or townhouse, and closer to her work would also be closer to me. She wouldn't have the upkeep of a house. Less stress means a longer life.

Would she really want to live near her fag son?

How can I tell her something like this; something that she has been told is wrong even longer than I have? How did this happen to me? How? I did everything that I was supposed to do! I was the good kid, the one that followed all of the rules. I'm supposed to be doing great now! I'm supposed to be successful, have a wife, and a kid. None of that is me, though.

I have a job, so that's something. I hate kids. And, well apparently I don't give that much thought to women.

-Damn it!

My fist feels little of the pain that it should as it meets the back of my car. A warm liquid finds its way over the top of my knuckles, falling backwards towards my arm. The blood seems excessive, but I can attribute that to the near constant drinking over the past two days. That was stupid. I open the driver-side car door and fall into the seat.

A watery blur overtakes my eyes in the mild light cast from the overhead bulb in my car, so I close them for a moment. A scan of the car only yields a button-down shirt I had worn to work a few days earlier and some old papers. I grab the shirt and wrap it around my hand tightly. My knuckle hurts and I hope that it is not broken. I'm sure it isn't; I don't have enough force to break my hand. Never been much of the punching type. Mostly, I think, because I have always assumed I would be bad at it.

This night has turned out to be a complete train wreck. Of course it is; my predictions have come true.

Predictions or lack of self-control?

I pull the visor down and look into the mirror. My eyes are red and glazy. I don't even know how I made the drive out here safely. The self-accusations begin immediately.

Did I make it safely? Did I do something wrong?

Stop. There's no use to worry yourself. You didn't hurt anyone.

I reach into the passenger seat with my good hand and pull another beer from the case. I'm not even sure what this conversation with myself has accomplished. I open the can and take a long, cold gulp.

-What now?

2:25AM, Monday

I'm not exactly sure how I have made it as far as I have, but here I am, walking down the side of what can only be called a farm road. Is this the side? Maybe it's the center. The tracks have grown over as it is hardly used for anything, if anything at all. I know where I am headed, but there are no memories to be remembered tonight about how I arrived at this decision. I could have brought my car, but I didn't. Walking seemed more appropriate, quieter. He shouldn't know that I am coming.

That doesn't really make much sense.

Perhaps to take my time. I'm not even sure why I'm nervous. It's been years, yet I don't even know how to talk to an apparition. I didn't know how to talk to the man that had lived in the same house with me, either.

My breathing has deepened and I sit down on the ground, pulling another can of beer from my coat pocket. The can clinks against the rocks on the road and I fall backwards, quickly, before I even realize what's happening.

-That's definitely going to hurt later, I mumble and laugh.

An enormous cloud moves briskly across the sky, stars falling behind and then reappearing moments later. It's beautiful. It's peaceful. I find myself longing for peace. The idea of getting up tomorrow, or I suppose today now, is more than I think that I can face at this point. Either way, I'm not going in tomorrow. I don't care if I get fired.

I'm so tired of the depression; the disquiet. It's found a way to consume every inch of me. My body hurts, and I'm exhausted. I just want to sleep all the time. I'm not sure I have even realized what it is until now. Alcohol is not the answer. I know that, but it's really opened my eyes tonight. I'm so fucking drained, so over all of the fighting.

I roll onto my stomach. It's the only way that I am going to be able to get up. My back is wet and I stumble to my feet grabbing the can of beer on my way back up. The same peaceful cloud has overtaken the moon and seems to be spinning. It's no longer a haunting reminder of beauty, simply haunting, a reminder that all lights eventually burn out.

The muted light from the moon behind is enough for me to continue forward into the night. If I was sober, I would be more worried about the dangers that could befall a human in the middle of nowhere at night. Coyotes, wolves.

I don't know. Maybe an accident like that would make things easier. No one would have the memory that I was sick and tired of going on.

Does being eaten sound better, I laugh.

It's hard to tell how long it would take to find me. My car is back at the house, though, so probably not that long. All of these dramatic theories. It's only mildly funny. I'm sure it wouldn't even warrant a blip on the radar of those who didn't know me. It probably won't even make a dent in the lives of those that do. My guess is it would take a while for my *friends* to even hear anything about it.

Someone would eventually post about it on Facebook, and then the pity train would roll into town. Those who talked to me once would post stories of our time together. Death, or more accurately the funeral, is nothing but a morose sideshow for the living.

Everything is blurry, and the pain in my throat is escalating quickly. Another gulp, another moment of relief. The moon finds its way through the fog and the old road opens up even further in front of me than before. I'm probably just noticing the extreme difference from the darkness. A pressure builds around my ears muffling the sound of the wind in the trees, and I can't decide if I find it soothing or destructive. My whole world is muffled.

There's little more than a fragile mind left within me. A complacent soul that has never been one for complacency. Who knows how they are going to deal with tragedy until they are forced into the situation? You can repeat the 'I'm fines' over and over again, to the world and to yourself, but the subconscious isn't one to listen to reasoning. In fact, I've found that mine is a self-destructive force. It wants me dead. It wants me to suffer. That is the only conclusion that I have about the matter. It wants to stop dealing as much as I think I do.

There is some kind of a fight between my heart, my soul, and my brain, and I'm not sure which is the strongest. My soul is terrified that I have done something unforgiveable, while my heart says that it's okay to be who you are, to find love in this world, and my brain, my brain tells me that life is one big joke. Life is something that really doesn't matter in the long run.

My brain tells me a lot of things like this in drunken stupors. It's the piece of me that's looking for a way out, a way to just stop all the other emotions. It's the one part of me that never stops moving when I drink. The soul knows that it will go on once it all stops and my brain will cease to continue, so ultimately, it's the stronger of the two. The winner. It's really a conundrum to me how they should coexist in the same body. One is so completely finite, while the other is the very definition of infinity.

The heart, it seems in this scenario, is of no real significance. It gets you into a lot of trouble, and as I have come to find, has lead me down a variety of paths that I wish I could come back from. I'm quickly finding that I am not one of those people that feels like my past has defined me and has made me a better person. If anything, I have let my past point me in the wrong direction too many times in an attempt to hurt myself.

I guess it all boils down to what is the reason for all of this? Have I developed a hatred for myself knowing what I have become, or have I let the views of others that didn't care enough to love me outweigh my own worth?

There was a time that I was so happy and on fire for God that I didn't care what anyone thought about me. I hear that I was such a strong child, so where did that change along the way? This cyclical process that is high school never stops and eventually leaves you so beaten down that you do in fact care more about what others think.

God is stronger than all of that.

I know that. But, I'm not strong. Right now, that's the only thing that I can fully grasp. I am too weak to overcome these problems.

Please, God, forgive me. Help me see a way out of the pain, out of this misery.

Life has simply become a popularity contest, or basically, how much ass you can kiss to get ahead. I don't want to be that person. I have never wanted to be that person, and when it happens, there's just more reason to hate myself.

I just want to be who I am. That probably comes off as stubborn and entitled, but why is it wrong to want to enjoy my life?

This all sounds like an anthemic pop song brainstorming session. It's almost too ridiculous to consider, but does that make it wrong? To want to actually enjoy my job, spending my days enjoying what I do? It's the place that I spend most of my time.

If that can't happen, then I have to go back to my brain and think then what if life is nothing but one big joke? A job is not your life, but it kind of is when you're first starting out. You work overtime, and stay on hour after hour to make sure that you do get ahead.

-No one gets out alive, I mutter, amused with myself that I can even remember that quote at this point in the night. I don't even really remember where it's from or who said it.

I trip over my own foot and stagger forward a few inches, trying desperately to save myself and my beer from colliding with the ground once again. There's only one can left in my left pocket and this one will need to last. A plan is the last thing in action and it's hard to tell how this is all going to take. My hand grazes the outside of my pocket to make sure my backup drink is in its place, and I realize I have chosen the wrong pocket and pull my phone out.

It's been hours and no one has gotten back to me. It's typical, and I'm not sure why I have spent so much time over the years dwelling and thinking about why this happens. I need to accept it as a fact of life. Everyone is always looking out for themselves. Even the most altruistic person will choose themselves in the end, but isn't that what I've been telling myself tonight? Sometimes you need to put yourself first in order to live. Making others happy is always a suicide mission.

That's stupid, and I know somewhere in the back of my mind that it's not true. I've seen many times that people will put others before themselves. I even know that it's been done many times for me, but I'm ungrateful. I want adoration from strangers. I don't know what that's about, either. I don't think I have come to one conclusion tonight on any of the questions popping up. If anything, there are more, and the deeper they go, the more the lack of answers hurts. I'm not sure that I want to answer them all, either.

There are so many things that I don't know or understand about myself, and that is a frustrating point for those who do care about me.

How do they think I feel then? Do they think it's fun for me to live with all of these unanswered questions?

They want me to explain how I'm feeling and why I'm so frustrated and self-destructive, but I can't answer it. Questions innumerate, voices transferring from life to my brain. So, I smile.

I've become very good at pretending that my life is fine. I tell them all that I'm great when really I couldn't care less about leaving my house or dealing with people. Most of my anxiety comes from the fact that I have to actually deal with other humans on a day to day basis. Well, those who really know me, the one or two, know when I'm upset. Maybe I don't hide it well at all, and those who don't see it, couldn't care less how I am really feeling.

That's life, I'm fully aware, but it's not the life that I care to live anymore. It's a lot easier to just smile and say that I'm fine than the questions that come with a negative response. I'm negative a lot of the time, I would say, especially tonight, but I'm beat. It's so irritating answering the same questions over and over. Why can't you be happy? There are people a lot worse off than yourself. Suck it up, buttercup.

People always know the right thing to say. Ha!

It's easier just to lie. I know that's not right, lying should not be my go-to; I know that. At least, I think I know that.

What if the answer is that I'm not a good person?

The rocky, overgrown lane abruptly ends with a manicured lawn expanding further into the darkness. The gray headstones rise off in the distance. In the blackness, there is the essence of some pagan land in Britain. My eyes are blurry, and the shadows cast by each of the stones throws me off as I try to maneuver around them. Finding the exact grave I'm looking for proves harder than I thought it would be at the beginning of this journey.

I reach for my phone and turn on the flashlight. My father is somewhere near the middle, beneath some kind of pine tree that I don't know the name. It doesn't look like any Christmas evergreen that I have seen, and to be honest, I'm not even sure if it is considered part of the pine family. What do I really know about trees, though?

Where are you, Dad?

The sirens had woken me for the second time that morning, the first of which I had not given much thought. I heard vomiting in the bathroom, but I had just assumed that my father had gone on another of his benders. It wouldn't be the first time I had heard him in the guest bathroom throwing up, making some extra work for himself to not let my mom know that he had driven home drunk. Again.

He never gave her credit for much, but she wasn't stupid.

It seemed a little later than usual but it required little force for me to fall back asleep. I heard him say something about a headache and his face going numb, but getting in the way of his hangover was not something I planned to do that morning. That was a mistake I had made enough times that I wouldn't let it happen again. He wasn't an abusive man, not in the physical sense, but he could definitely make you feel like shit about yourself.

-Hey, Dad.

It had taken a bit, but now his headstone stood in front of me. It seems smaller in the dark, eclipsed by some of the more extravagant statues of decades past. Our family subscribes to the knowledge that a soul leaves the body once death has occurred, and nothing more than a body is left behind. There's no need to erect a monument to something as finite as the human body.

His grave marker is simple and gray, bearing his name and years of birth and death. My mother's name stands next to his, bearing only her birth year. For some reason, this brings forth even more anxiety, my chest tightening. I even look away for a moment, scared to acknowledge the inevitability of it all.

I hadn't heard the thud of my father hitting the floor, or my mother crying into the phone. I don't even know if that's how it happened. It's not something we discuss, because, how do you bring that up? Death is a tricky subject matter. There is no one way to handle it, and pushing someone to deal with it in the same way that you would is not fair to them. No two people are the same; they can be very similar, and there is only a numerable amount of responses, but no two are the exact same.

It had been so sudden, so unexpected. Aneurysm. I had typed that word into the internet so many times, waiting for the phone line to sync and give me even the slightest information, just trying to understand exactly what had happened. It's so difficult for a teen, or I guess anyone, to understand why they weren't good enough for a parent, but when that parent is suddenly removed from the picture, how do you move on?

When you've heard your father worried that you are going to become the worst thing you can become in the eyes of a conservative countryman, how do you live with yourself? How do you look at yourself every day and think that you are good enough for anyone?

-How are you doing, Dad?

I know this is stupid to talk to the dead. I know they are gone from this place. This body will only disintegrate into dust, into nothing.

It's hard to take it all so seriously, when what we do here on Earth really means nothing in the whole scope of things.

I'm not talking from a Christian standpoint, but from a business one. Why do we spend so much time trying to be successful, losing people along the way, just so we can all end up the same?

There was an illusion that I had been strong after this sudden death. I had put on a smile, using humor and praying constantly. God had pulled me through this hard time. I thought I had moved past, accepted that these things do happen. But, now, here I am standing face to face with a gravestone, drunk, in the middle of the night. Where have I gone wrong? Do I spend too much time thinking about the past? Did I never actually let it go?

And why, why can't I let it go?

-Who knew we would end up so much alike, right? I'm sure that is probably the worst thing that you could hear right now, if you knew what was going on. I think I need this, though. I need to talk to you, to make peace with it all. Maybe it's even time to join you.

At first, I thought the sirens must be on television. We don't get those out here in the country. I figured my dad had settled into his recliner in front of the TV with a can of beer to push away the sting of the hangover from the night before. I had laid there in my bed thinking about what I could do that day. I needed to get out of the house or stay in my room. It wasn't until the sirens seemed louder that our old TV could go that I began to worry. When the brakes screeched into the driveway, I threw my blankets to the side and walked to the window, still hoping this was all a mistake.

I'm honestly not sure what I expected to see. Had my father driven drunk and hurt someone? It was an ambulance, though. Not a cop. I had heard my mother yell something from the front porch and grabbed a tee shirt from the floor beside my bed. I wanted to run out of the room and down the stairs, but I couldn't move faster than a walk. I slowly opened my door, trying desperately to hear what was going on downstairs. It would be better to be prepared.

There was so much screaming, so much action, so much everything that there was no feasible way for me to put any of it together. I walked to the landing and looked down into the entryway. Shadows moved swiftly against the hardwood floor.

-My son, I have to get my son! We'll meet you at the hospital! Should I go with him? Can we both fit into the ambulance with you, her voice climbed and staggered.

It had gotten quiet then. The silence was sudden, and it was startling. My mother's cry filled up that silence moments later. I knew it wasn't good. No one was yelling anymore, and no one seemed to be rushing.

What do I do?

I wasn't the man of the house. As far as he was concerned, I was going to be gay. Being gay was not being a real man. I was just going to be a fag that amounted to nothing with my school plays. He had been drunk, trashed off his ass, when he went on these rants, but I can't say that that made it any better. The man I looked up to was saying horrible things about me. The person that was supposed to show me how to be a real man had failed and then left me to figure it out on my own. He had left my mother to figure out her life on her own.

-You left us to fend for ourselves! How is that fair, Dad? How? You destroyed our self-worth and then bam, you left us.

My mother had been of the stay-at-home variety, the picture of what my dad thought a woman should be, and then he was gone. She had to find a way to salvage our family and keep us from losing what little we had. My father had spent his last years working as a logger, and not knowing, or needing to know, much about it at the time, he had no insurance. The funeral had been simple, just a few people at our small Methodist church a few miles down the road from the house.

That service had been on a Saturday, and she had to start looking for a job on Monday.

There wasn't time for her to grieve or process what had happened. Mom knew that she didn't have a choice, she was the one that had to take care of the family now.

-Do you know that she found a job in three days, Dad? Three. Do you understand what you ignored? What you had with her? I know you don't! Even as a child, I could tell that wasn't what love was about. That wasn't what love was supposed to be. You didn't want anything to do with us, did you? Sometimes—sometimes I wonder why you even married, had a kid. Was it obligation? Did you really want it at the time?

I understand the need to be alone. It's why I spend most of my time like that.

Is it? Are you really lying to yourself now, Ez?

-I've spent 25 years telling myself that I wanted love and the last three that that is the last thing that I want.

You're losing your mind.

If only that were true. Madness makes for a far better story, don't you think? Go out in flames.

It's one way to be remembered.

What is it that scares me the most? People not liking me or not being remembered once I am gone. I haven't done anything particularly special, and I don't want to be remembered for all the pain that it would cause, no matter to how few that pain would extend. Perhaps I am being selfish. How much love does one person need? We don't need adoration. That only leads to pride and falling on your face. I only need the love of God.

-God.

It's a whisper and silent prayer. Can you forgive me for the mess that I have made out of my life? Can you forgive the fact I cannot control how I feel?

-You were right, Dad. I'm gay. You've got a fag for a son!

The rumbling in my stomach is familiar and I turn away from my father's stone to vomit. I'm sure if he were here, this would be the identical reaction that he would have. I can't say for sure though.

-Dad, how could you leave me like this, feeling unloved, unwanted? You probably didn't mean to, but I don't know! I need answers!

Each word echoes back to me in a slightly less ragged yell than the one that left my mouth seconds before. Then, in a whisper:

-I can't blame you for this. I'm my own man. I need to move on, but I can't. I'm not strong. I'm lonely and I'm weak.

Make it all go away. I want the world to stop. My world.

I sit on the ground and my head hits his stone. After a few seconds of stillness, there is still no warm liquid falling onto my face or neck so I hope for the best that there is no bleeding, at least anything substantial.

-Remember when we'd play hide and seek out here when I was little? Did you know we did that, Dad? Probably not. We'd hide behind gravestones and trees. Some might find it inappropriate, but it was fun.

I've never been scared of cemeteries, and I wonder if I can attribute it to the fact it was basically our playground. At work, we have the most random conversations, and one of them had been about graveyards and how most people were freaked out by them. I guess I don't take much time to think about what's just beneath the surface. Each one of these outlines is a person that used to have a life, used to be loved.

Well, I assume still loved. It gets to the point, though, where the memory begins to fade and future generations won't even know who they were, other than a picture in a photo album or a story. They won't know their struggles, or their personalities. Eventually, these past generations are just a name on a family tree on a website that reveals those who came before.

Maybe I treat life like it is one big cemetery. Perhaps we all do. Each face that you don't know is a stranger, someone going through their own shit, and we don't care to know what that is. Each person has enough of their own problems, so why would they take on another?

Good people do. They do what they can to help. They try to figure out why people act the way they do, and if something is wrong, something is off, they go out of their way to make that problem go away, or at least alleviate it in some small way. I feel like maybe at some point I was like that. Somewhere in the past.

Some days I believe there are shades of my old self coming out, but then they disappear behind witty sarcasm that brings a laugh, but not always contentment. I equate laughter with feelings of familiarity and friendship, but that's only a surface level, fucked up way of going about the world. You can make a stranger on the street laugh; you don't have any sort of personal connection, yet this is how I see myself. I'm the comedian, and if the laughter stops then there is nothing left of me but the madness, the crazy thoughts that fill my head. The random song lyrics, the stupid stories.

But aren't those quirks who I am? Are they really bad? I love the fact that I have a great sense of humor.

Had I been born rich, it wouldn't be considered crazy. It would, but it would be accepted as trailblazing and unique. Instead, I'm left with the awkward, blank stares that illustrate just how little my friends understand. I think some of my friends keep me around because they know that I'm clumsy and I'm on the edge of a cliff, and I could fall at any time. A fall would then give them the chance to say that they made efforts to help, but it was too much. The sympathy for them would overcome their sense of need with no effort put in to help in the first place. Watch the man die with no attempt to reach out an arm, but soak up the soothing words because you were forced to watch him go.

I am weird.

I think that I just proved that. I also think that I am a nice guy that doesn't want other people to suffer, and if there is something that I can do to help, I will do it. It's a shame that my unusual character traits overshadow any goodness that I can do. I'm not one to go about bragging about my good deeds. I don't think that is something that God wants from us. He wants us to help, and He will be the one to bless us.

Even my thoughts are rambling tonight. None of this really makes sense, but it does. To me, it all makes perfect sense.

I'm tired and want to sleep.

-Have you had time to process all of this yet, Dad? Do you hate me now? What will your friends think? I guess it doesn't matter because they don't come around anymore. Another thing we have in common, I scoff.

I continue: We are both very good at allowing people into our lives that rolled with the good times but were nowhere to be found when you actually needed them.

What a lonely existence we have cultivated for ourselves. Maybe that's why he was so closed off to us. It's hard to accept love when it has been denied so many times. Maybe, we're both just fucked up in the head. It would almost be comforting if that were the case, that this was natural, that there was no cure for it. I could accept it then, go about my days knowing there was truly no difference to be made no matter how much harder we all tried.

I know there's help, though; there's always help. I think.

I reach for the can that I have placed on the bottom lip of the stone. The realization that no more liquid remains is a hard one. I pull my arm back to throw the can in anger but think better of it, letting the can fall to the ground just beside me. My head jerks to the left at a soft thud. There is nothing in the light of my phone as I shine it back and forth around me. There was a time when I would say that I believed in ghosts. That part of me has gone now. If anyone were to come back due to some unfinished business, it would definitely have been my father. He seemed so unhappy all of the time.

Sometimes, I wish he would have shared more with my mother and me. Just let us know what was going on. Was he hurting?

I have blocked out much of my childhood, but who knows if it was out of necessity or the fact that my mind is shot these days. I have begun to forget things, to lose simple words from the tip of my tongue. I'm not sure that I can contribute it to aging because if that were the case, I can't begin to imagine what my latter half of life would look like. I do know that sharing his feelings was not something that my dad wanted. The knowledge I have of his childhood might as well be the knowledge I have of the next person I pass on the street.

Maybe I was the selfish one who never asked. How much can you expect from a child?

I unroll the sleeves to my shirt to provide some more coverage. I'm not sure if this warm streak has worn off or if it's the alcohol that's losing its touch. Deeper and extensive exhaustion take hold and I look in the direction of my old house, my mom, and the past. Thinking about walking back now seems too overwhelming, too much of a journey to undertake in the middle of the night. I can't even consider the amount of alcohol that I have let into my system today. Sometimes, I think that alcohol poisoning is a myth because if it were real, then I surely would have died from it already.

My body is aching, I'm tired, and my nose is starting to feel congested. The area around my knees is throbbing.

-I’m so damn tired.

2:50AM, Monday

It's impossible to pinpoint the exact moment at which I passed out but looking down at my phone, it couldn't have been for more than 15 minutes. I feel surprisingly well, or sober I should say, for such a short time. My head feels clear. That's impossible I realize, but I do feel better in this regard. The headache has taken full effect, however, and that's the only thing on my mind, currently. The struggle to stand takes much longer than it should. I look down at the stone, thinking, wondering.

-You've had a bit to think on it now, Dad. So, how do you feel? Am I the huge failure you figured I would be?

I know there are no answers to be had here, but I needed to get it out. Needed to talk it aloud with someone who couldn't judge me. Turns out that person was the person I feel had judged me the most in life.

-I love you, Dad. No matter what, I do. There were times that I wanted to be anywhere else than in your presence, but now and then I still miss you. When I have a question about my car, or how something works, I wish you were here to answer it for me. Do you think that maybe that would have given you some happiness, to teach me something that you considered manly? I know I'm never going to get the answers I'm looking for, so I guess that I should accept that, right? Or, I need to do something about it.

I grab my empty beer can from the ground and turn to walk towards the field and overgrown road behind me. For a moment, I stop and think and finally decide to take the main road instead; it's closer to me, and I don't think I have the energy to dodge all the overgrown plant life. There are no headlights, and that seems right. It should be cold, the roads should be icy and snowy, but the sudden warming has eliminated all of that.

-Most people are smart enough to know that they have work this morning, too.

I'm not one of those people.

I feel like I should care more about the fact that I would normally be waking up in three hours, but that is the last thing on my mind. I don't care if I ever go back to that office again. I'm tired of the bullshit, the kissing ass that my bosses seem to want me to do, the fact that no one seems to do their job and nothing ever happens. Corporate America has sucked the life out of me, and I just don't care anymore.

I'm annoying myself tonight with all of this over-analysis. If I were a shrink, I would hand myself the razor and say go for it. I am blaming so much on outside influences, but I know that my feelings come from me.

Why can't I figure it all out?

I probably need sleep, but then what? Nothing ever really seems clearer in the morning. Who came up with that saying, anyway? I end up tossing and turning, weighing every outcome in my mind, and then I get an hour of sleep. My body feels like crap and I'm no closer to solving the problem. I'm a fucking mess. I know that.

The breeze has picked up and the way it intersperses with what's left of the dead corn stalks make a whistling sound. It's familiar, and it eases the tension in my shoulders some. They drop to a natural level, no pressure. I hear the beginnings of a vehicle coming, though I cannot tell from behind or ahead. I close my eyes and continue to walk. This goes on for a minute before I hear the blasting horn and I open them. A car swerves around me but does not stop. I have stumbled into the actual lane.

I'm not sure that I wanted to die at this moment, but I wanted to see how it felt. The idea of dying, the idea of pure peace.

Would it be peace? Or would I burn?

-Too many questions.

I don't even know if I need answers anymore. I just want it all to be done. The pain to stop. The stupid decisions to stop.

My decisions are a choice, and I should be able to halt them in my head, but depression found a way in through the emotional abuse, and it's a self-destructive force like none I've ever seen. The punishment that I place on myself is far worse, I believe, than anyone else could deem to achieve. There is no greater critic of my faults, or hell even my triumphs. It's no wonder that I have so very few people in my life that care; I have the neediness of a five-year-old.

This comes out extensively in my drunken stupors, and inevitably, those people get lives, grow up, and they walk away.

Now, I make sure that I'm the one to walk away first. That way, it's my decision.

-I'm what I've got, and it's me that needs to make this decision. Tonight. It has to be tonight.

The booze and depression have fought and loved one another throughout the night, and in this moment of their collision I can only picture an empty room. An ugly room, paneled top to bottom with a popcorn ceiling. The box at the front is blue; gross, discolored blue. It's not something that I ever would have chosen, but I guess a funeral is not for the one who is dead.

It’s for the ones that are left behind, to dwell in the grief.

That’s not right. It’s meant to alleviate the destruction that death has upon a person’s soul, to make it real. If it’s real, then you have no choice but to deal with it head on.

There’s much denial that one can find themselves in following a tragic event, no mandatory rule that you have to deal with these emotions, but ultimately, if you don’t, it will take every good emotion, gesture, thought that you have and twist it into something not quite right. You detach from the world around you, and love seems like something for everyone but you. You can find someone to spend your life with, but if you never let go, then ultimately you’re alone.

Get it together. This is just a moment in time, albeit a bad one. It's not the worst moment. It's insignificant.

Is that how I really feel, or is that just the booze talking?

I look around the room that I have constructed in my head, each empty chair a reminder of each individual that I have let walk out of my life because I didn’t care enough to fight for them. I’m not even sure if it’s my own doing at this point. I know that the perception of who I have become is a great fall from where I have come, but many of those who have that perception walked away long before that. The lights are low to hide the corners of the makeup that has been applied to my own face. It doesn't look natural, but of course, who would be the better judge of that than the person that had to look into those eyes every single day?

My feet are starting to hurt, and I can't really decide how close I am to my house. I need a break and I let myself fall onto the ground and lay back onto the road. I'm sure I will hear if another car approaches, but then I'm not one hundred percent sure that I would want to move out of the way.

-Could I do that to another person?

Could I let someone take on the guilt of killing me when it was completely intentional on my part? It's almost a certainty that the cops would rule it an accident. They would do a blood test and assume that I was too drunk to know what I was doing. That would be easier on my family. A tragic accident is always a little easier than believing that a loved one wanted to take their own life. I'm not even sure what makes it so difficult for those behind. If I'm being completely honest with myself, I can't think that I have truly known someone to take their own life.

Is it the fact that they couldn't save the person? Or is it that their love wasn't enough to keep them going? I suppose there is no one answer to what haunts people so much about suicide. Sometimes, people just can't do it anymore. One day they decide that they just want to stop feeling anything.

I'm here. I'm to this point, and it's not something I ever thought would happen to me. I woke up Saturday morning. I was rested and I was content. By the end of the night, everything had spiraled out of control and now I am laying in the road.

There are very few people who could find the humor in this situation, but I'm one of them. The one with the sense of humor that others don't understand. I think it's easier to understand the darker things in life when you've lost someone close to you at a young age. I mean close as in a parent, or child, or whomever. I can't believe that I am rambling this much. Usually, I am in need of an audience to keep this going for hours. I'm practically on my own nerves, but the thoughts won't stop.

The pavement is cold and hard, but I can't find the strength to get up. I want to sleep, but I can't go out this way. There would be too many questions left for my mother, and I don't think that I can do that to her. If I am going to do this, then I need to do it right.

Is there really a right way to do it? I need to leave a letter. I need to let her know that she had nothing to do with this decision and that I love her more than anything. I need her to understand that this is on me.

-I don't want to go to hell.

More questions arise than I was prepared to answer, or more accurately, ask myself. The fear of hell for loving someone in an intimate way that I'm only supposed to love as a brother disintegrated any other reasons that could damn my own soul. How do you choose between two mortal sins according to religion? Do I sacrifice happiness to stay alive and continue to deny myself the joy that my heart tells me that I want, or do I sacrifice my soul to show that I am willing to give up the slow destruction of it?

-God, I really need You right now. I have no idea what I'm doing.

I feel like I should be crying, but I'm so tired, so worn out, that nothing happens. I'm not even sure if the word tired begins to describe where I'm at. My body doesn't want to move. Part of me wishes that God would just have mercy on me and take me now.

-Lord, I know that I've fallen so short of what You want from me, but please I need You now. I don't think I can go on like this. Can you forgive me?

The speed of the wind has increased and somehow the temperature seems to have risen once again. My sleeves get rolled up again. I thought it would slack off and fall back to the frigid morning temperatures of yesterday but it's just something else that I've been wrong about. I wonder if anyone has seen any of my texts. I pull my phone from my pocket and the screen illuminates. The battery has not died, which comes as a surprise.

Nothing. No messages, no calls. No concern. I probably shouldn't have sent out any texts. That's just asking for the guilt to start for them tomorrow. Today, I mean. I've drunk texted them all one too many times, so it's reasonable there would be no answer.

I pull up a game I've been playing and take my turn. It feels wrong to leave it unfinished. What happens when they play again and nothing ever comes back? Should I tell them? Send a message.

-You're so stupid, I admonish myself.

Why would they give a damn about what happens to a stranger?

Because it's human nature to care about others. That's what we do.

-You don't, Ez.

Yes, but I try. I care about different things than others, but I'm not going to coddle another adult.

Isn't that what I want?

It's not good for anyone. Life is life, and for the majority of it, it is boring or bad. The truly joyous moments are few in comparison, and I guess, I don't truly appreciate them. There's no guessing involved; I know that I don't give them the weight that they truly deserve.

I cannot seem to remember the last time that I felt that true joy in my heart. And I know that's on me. I haven't shown that gladness for the blessings that I have received. I continue to dwell in the sadness, closing off each passageway to something new and better. Every morning I try to find a reason to smile, and usually I do, until I find myself letting work destroy it.

We all need jobs, I understand that. I shouldn't complain and whine, but it's to myself, so does that really matter?

-Am I repeating myself? Are these the same things I've been turning over in my head all day?

Who even knows at this point? I finally find the strength and roll onto my stomach. My phone pushes into the underside of my stomach and hope I that I have not cracked the screen. Should tomorrow actually come for me, I don't want to have to spend hundreds to replace that in the morning. I find my way to my knees and I'm sure it's about as graceful as a baby trying to crawl for the first time.

It takes longer than I care to admit, but I finally find a firm footing back at the side of the road. No more vehicles have made their way past. Is this a sign that maybe I shouldn't go through with it?

I look for signs in things and make that statement about finding them, but are there really signs and how do you know which ones are accurate? The hidden driveway is not far from me now. Two old willows frame it, even in the darkness. It's taken nearly an hour for me to get back to this point.

∞

-So, what do I do, now, I stammer.

The side panel on my car shifts inward slightly as my back hits it hard. It feels good to look out over something familiar, even in darkness. It's comforting. This is home, and it always will be. Everyone has that place that they feel they belong. I don't need to see what's there. I already know it, each small hole in the earth, each bump, each rock. Everything. I could take off my shoes and run around barefoot without the worry of injury right now, even inebriated.

This is my home, my physical home on this Earth. That's never going to change. When they mention my death, this will be the place they list first. Mom will be the person by whom I am survived.

Hm. It's weird; I've never really put this thought into terms of print before. My life summed up in a few meager sentences, with no accomplishments. I'm sure they will fill out the space with plenty of filler, much like a college paper when you have no real grasp or care for the subject.

I imagine that most people my age would have a little more that could easily be transcribed into what most would call a good life. In fact, I see my friends announcing their engagements and pregnancies all over the internet. Me. Well, apparently I'm just finding myself for the first time. Not that today is the first time I have spent questioning myself, but this is the first time that I have managed to let the words fill the air around me.

-Maybe I should figure out who I am before I stop, I slur.

I'm pretty sure it should be a stopping point when I can actually hear the intoxication in my own voice. It makes sense though. I should take the time to get to know myself before I decide that giving up is the route that I should take.

Am I too old for that, now? To restart?

I'm too old to reinvent myself, to go through figuring out who I am all over again. This is something that you do in your late teens and early twenties, and here I am nearly 30, asking myself who the hell I am.

-Why?

Why couldn't I have been braver when I was growing up, coming into the person that I wanted to be? Why couldn't it have been acceptable? Why did I have to spend so many years ashamed of what I was and the feelings that I didn't want to get out? I pushed everything away and let those around me come into a life of nothing but lies.

Not lies, but my biggest secret, one that could have brought me happiness if I had embraced it, was kept deep inside. There was no real need to keep it. I could have stopped lying. Is that where all of that began? The storytelling. I became so good at being someone else that I can't even figure out who I am now.

-Damn it!

My elbow meets metal and I grab it immediately. That was stupid. Fucking stupid.

Where is the sun? Daylight should have been here hours ago, but still nothing but pure darkness. I reach for my phone. There is a message, finally a message. Tank? What does he want? Did I text him? I don't even remember at this point. I don't even remember his real name.

-Dude, can I get a ride home?

Should have known. No one reaches out unless there is something I can do for them. What about all the nights I'm sitting at home, alone, wondering if everyone is busy. I sit there, watching television, bored. Perhaps that is the key to a happy life—boredom. Learn to accept that not every moment can be exciting, and that those are something to be treasured and held onto during the bad.

I plan events, fun things, so that I have something to look forward to just to keep myself going. Is this how it is for everyone? Is it depression? It's not something that you really talk about as a kid. You aren't told that most of you are going to have menial jobs and you have to find a way to live with yourself.

Most people haven't spent years telling everyone they know lies; they are guilt-free about what they have done. I long for the absolution of forgiveness, but there is no guarantee that what I am is forgivable. That scares me beyond what I can explain. I love God, I have been saved, but this part of me won't go away. I have prayed so hard to make it go away.

It's not wrong to love someone, is it? I've spent so many years looking for someone to look past the bad and see the good. I want to be loved, but this roadblock has always been there. I don't even see it when girls like me. I continue to feel invisible and maybe that is a good thing. If I am invisible, I can't give into the urges like I have already done tonight.

How can drinking numb the pain yet make it so much worse in the end? How can it make you feel so good about yourself but then drop you at the last minute to your lowest point? Lord, this is such a mess, the way that I have lived my life. I need to figure something out because tomorrow will be here soon. I either need to sleep or—who knows. I need to get up, that is the first thing.

I roll onto my stomach again, thankful that no one is here to see me like this and crawl to the back of my car. There are no lights on within the house, so my mother has not realized her idiot son is sitting outside drunk off his stupid ass. I need to leave before she freaks out on me. I can't handle a lecture tonight. It would be nice to say goodbye, though. Hug her one last time. I don't want to see the look of disappointment as the last look that she gives me. I want to remember her smiling like the last time I saw her.

-Goodbye, I whisper.

Is that it? Have I made my decision? I push my body to a wobbling position on my feet, letting the car do most of the work holding me upright. It takes a couple of tries, but I push myself off and walk towards the porch. I fall and hit my knee on the two stairs but manage to keep myself quiet.

-What a damn shitshow.

I look at my hand; the blood has pooled out around the fabric.

-Damn.

I forgot that I'd even hurt it. I must be drunker than even I realize. I don't remember why I forced myself over to the porch. I look around, slam my hands into my pockets. I have no pen, no paper. Only my thoughts; what good does that do?

I pull my phone out once again, staring at the screen trying to figure out what the multiple question marks mean in the previous text message. Oh, yeah. Someone had wanted a ride. I'm definitely in no shape to be giving anyone a ride tonight. I'm surprised that I made it out here without killing myself.

Pull it together, Ezra! You have to drive one more time. The drive is longer than I think is possible, but I need it. I need to make sure that this clarity is actually real and not something brought on by hours of drinking. I need to think it out. I need to talk it out.

There's no one to talk it out with, though. It's just me and my head, which funny enough, is the reason that I am even at this point.

No, that's not right. My heart. My heart is the reason that I am here tonight, questioning everything about myself. There are so many quotes about the heart and feelings, but I can't think of one right now.

I've spent too much time thinking tonight, today, whatever the hell it is at this point. I feel as if I should sleep, but I'm wide awake. Maybe if I just lay down, I'll actually go to sleep. That would be the end of all of this. The sun would wake me up, I'd get my lecture from Mom, and I'd continue on. But, can I keep up with this lie? I’m emotionally exhausted. I want nothing more than to stop. Stop.

-Stop, I mumble.

This should not be my decision.

Just go there. You know you think best when you are there.

My intake of air seems more like a gasp than a breath in my attempt to stand. I hit my knee again but ignore the pain that has now spread to the rest of my leg.

-What the hell is wrong with you, Ezra?

I turn quicker than I ought to and the world around me begins to turn, quickly, and I nearly fall down.

-How did you let yourself get like this?

-AJ?

-Yeah, dude. Now, answer me.

-I can honestly say that I have never been this fucking drunk before.

-You’re a mess.

-And you’re a damn imaginary friend.

-So, who’s the crazy one here?

-It’s me, I think we both know that. You came from my head. You said it yourself, I’m a mess.

-It’s fixable.

-Ya think?

-I know.

-You’re a lot more optimistic than I remember. Did I make you this annoying, or is that something that evolved?

-Evolved? I just say what you're thinking, Ez.

-I didn't even know that you could have hallucinations when you were drunk.

-Maybe you just needed someone to talk to, and you were sick of talking to yourself.

-Talking to yourself gets you nowhere. At least, for me. I spend either too much or too little on a decision and either way, it usually finds its way into a pile of shit.

-Then stop it.

-Thanks, ass. Goodnight.

I stagger to the car and open the door quickly. I'm not sure if the speed was to keep myself from falling or to prove to myself that I am still capable of my own thoughts. That I can still control my own actions.

-Your fucking invisible friend is talking to you; I think we are way past the point that you should be driving, Ez.

I shouldn't have driven at all tonight. I shouldn't be out here in the middle of nowhere, but I can't seem to stop myself. I need to be alone, but I don't want to be alone. I'm sure it's actually the other way around.

It takes a moment for me to raise my arm to turn the key. I pull the gearshift into reverse and close one eye to better focus on the scene just outside the back window, then pull off slowly. The air around my vehicle seems hazy now, a vast difference from when I first pulled in. I lean forward and realize that I have forgotten to turn on my headlights.

Once the vehicle comes to a stop at the highway, I push the gearshift into park and turn off the headlights once again.

-You've got to pull it together.

There are a few beers left in the case, and I reach for another. It's a stupid idea, but I'm pretty sure the alcohol is the only thing that is keeping me going at this point.

-You don't want to kill someone else, do you, AJ asks.

-Shut up.

-You're being stupid.

-You're just the angel; my mind is the devil.

The burn from the liquid has grown less intense in my throat. Another gulp, and I swish the beer around in my mouth before finally swallowing. Just do it; it's a straight shot. Just one more 30-minute drive and you can stop for the night. I need to do it there if I am going to do it.

Does it even matter where?

I suppose not, but somehow it does. What's the point of going someplace that makes you happy just to end it? I suppose it's one last chance to be happy. The world has let you down, and you have taken it into your own hands. You can be happy one last time.

I can be happy one last time.

-So you've made your decision, AJ asks from the passenger seat.

-I think.

-That sounds convincing.

-Shut up.

The headlights shine brighter on the paved road than on the dirt. Just go! I hit the gas and swerve off the far side of the road slightly. I correct my mistake and watch the white lines intently, making sure to stay between them. The vehicle moves from to side to side quickly, like driving in a storm.

-Don't concentrate so hard, I berate.

Drive naturally. You're forcing it. I have found myself in solitude, not only inside the warmth of my car. The rumblings in my gut seem to make phantom sounds in my ear. The music is nearly maxed and I roll the window down. There's a freedom in the wind that I don't fully understand. I find that I can lose myself in it.

My headlights meet a green sign. Only 25 miles.

-Almost there.

5:52AM

- It's going to be okay, Ezra. It is.

-I'm not so sure about that.

-You know you don't have to go through with it, Matt says, pulling away and walking to the edge of the rock. It's a beautiful spot no matter what you decide.

-What are you talking about?

-Don't. We both know why you're out here in the middle of the night. The morning, now, I suppose.

He balances on one leg and lets the other float into the air above the rushing waterfall.

-What do you think it's going to be like, he continues after a moment. Your body is going to automatically try to save itself. It's not gonna be quick. Do you think you'll change your mind?

He leans out over the darkness, farther than what seems humanly possible.

-Because I don't think there is going to be any changing your mind once you're down there.

He seems wistful, contemplative, but the words are harsh. That's probably just me, though. I can feel my body trembling and I don't think the temperature has dropped.

-You don't know that's why I'm out here, I speak loudly, with faux conviction.

-I do.

-Why do you care?

-Why do you care if I know the truth? You just met me.

-What if you try to stop me?

-What if I do? Maybe, that's what you need, someone to stop you from doing this.

-That's not your choice.

-Is it yours?

-It's my life.

-What if God has more for you?

-What?

-Do you think because I smoke weed and drink that I don't believe?

-I mean—.

-That's just the preconceived notions of our religions. Some of them do more damage than they do good. Some of them spew outright hate.

-I don't think I'm like that. Is that how I seem?

-No, but I think that's what sent you out here tonight. The way you touched my hand. I think you're struggling.

-Why do you think you know me so well?

-Am I right?

Silence.

I let the back of my hand brush across the rough surface of the rock below me.

-Well?

-Yeah.

-God doesn't hate you. He loves everyone.

-I know.

-Do you really know?

-It's hard to think of it that way sometimes, when we do things that are condemned by a good portion of the religious community.

-He isn't religion. He's God.

-Do you ever feel like you're losing your mind?

-Do you think I'm crazy?

-No, I think that I might be.

-You don't seem like it. Just lost.

-Before you showed up, I was talking to my childhood imaginary friend. You might not even be real. That's how drunk I am.

He laughs and says: if I'm not, then you created me for a reason in your mind. Who knows, maybe it was God who sent me down here to talk some sense into you.

-So you don't think it's a good idea?

-It's up to you. I just want you to know that it's not your only option. There are other ways to deal with your sadness, your feelings of being lost.

-Right now I just want it all to stop. I don't want to feel anything. I've been drinking all day and my head hasn't stopped once.

-Then sleep. Take some time for yourself.

-I have a job.

-You're not going to have a job if you kill yourself, either. You can always find another one. Find yourself, dude. Or don't. Like I said, it's up to you. I'm just a concerned citizen.

He turns and falls into a sitting position beside me.

-Is that a laugh, he asks.

-I guess.

-See, you're not totally hopeless then. There's always something in this world to laugh about. Especially when you have a sick sense of humor like me.

He puts his arm around me and pulls me shoulder to shoulder with him.

-So, what's it going to be, sir?

-Really?

-Yeah. I'm tired and need to go to sleep. I want to be here to support you if you're going to make the jump, though. At least I can tell the police where to start the search in the morning.

Although, then there might be a lot of questions about what I could have done to stop you, and I would have had to be like I did everything I could. I would definitely give an onscreen interview to the news.

-You're a mess, I chuckle.

-That's true.

-What would you say in an interview?

-Well, clearly we would have been the best of friends. I would definitely need to take an extended period off from work to "grieve."

I can see him use his fingers to make the quotes in the air.

-You're kind of an asshole.

-It's part of my charm, bro.

-Yeah, it works for you.

-Are you hitting on me, again?

-Shut up, I say as I punch him in the arm.

-Kidding.

-I know.

-Okay, for real. Do it, or come over and camp with us. It's getting cold again, and I need to go sit by the fire.

-You go.

-Really? You're still thinking about doing it after that amazing speech I just gave you? It was filled with inspiration and laughter. It had everything.

-Oh geez.

-Come on, let's go to the fire.

-Is this part where you rob and kill me?

-I would just ask for your wallet and wait for you to jump at this point.

He stands and extends his hand.

-Let's go. You're not doing this. I decided for you. You're not ready. You're too cool of a guy to go out like this. Plus, if you are doing this over being gay, you haven't had a relationship yet, and you need to do that once before you die. That's when you'll really want to kill yourself, but it can be great.

The clouds open to reveal the moon, and I can finally make out his facial features. He looks like a frat boy turned lumberjack. Or hippie.

-Dude, let's go!

-What if it's supposed to end here?

-It's not.

-Fine.

I grab his hand and he pulls me from the ground.

-You smell like a distillery.

-You smell like a skunk.

Thank you to everyone who has supported me through all of my writings over the years. I know it can be difficult listening to my wild ideas. This book has been a work in progress for some time now and I hope that it can help others trying to find their way in this world. Thanks Mom, of course, for reading and editing (and your continued love), and Aunt Becky for always being there to push me forward. Tommy, Ashley, Amanda, and Meghan for believing in my writing even when I wasn't sure it was even passable as decent. Jonn, for taking me in like a stray dog and keeping me sane. And anyone I forgot, it was purely an oversight, and thank you as well! Without all of your support, I probably never would have finished this novel.

God bless,

Greg

Made in the USA
Columbia, SC
23 June 2020

11958145R00143